G000047866

KILLERS
ASSASSINS
& SPIES

by

George A Smith

About the Author

The author is a retired detective chief inspector and former head of Brighton CID. He was a senior investigating officer on many murder investigations. During his career he operated in the UK and Ireland with the Counter Terrorism Command. He was also recruited into the Security Service (MI5) and worked in the UK and USA with the FBI. As a young detective inspector he was involved in the interrogation of Argentine Commander Alfredo ASTIZ during the Falklands War. He has a BA degree in history and politics and is a keen photographer. In retirement he owns and manages a woodland in West Sussex.

All royalties from this novel are being donated to St. Catherine's Hospice (Crawley).
To find out more about the work of the hospice please visit:

www.stch.org.uk

CONTENTS

Chapter One

Arrival of an Assassin

*Recent years have witnessed the suspicious deaths
of Russian oligarchs resident in the United Kingdom. Subsequent investigations showed some had
been murdered on the orders of shadowy figures
in Moscow. Operation Backfire was established by
British Intelligence to deal with the latest threat.*

The cruise-ferry MV Bretagne departed the French
port of Saint-Malo on schedule at 20:30 hours for the
English south coast port of Portsmouth. An assassin, a
trained killer, posing as a passenger was on board. The
overnight sailing from the north coast of Brittany port
takes approximately eleven hours and was scheduled to
berth at the port of Portsmouth at 07:45 hours. It was a
calm, slightly chilly early autumn evening with a clear
blue darkening sky.

Prior to the departure, a dark green coloured Land Rover Defender truck was one of the last vehicles to drive onto the garage deck and park. In accordance with regulated safety procedures the driver applied the handbrake, placed it in first gear and, on exiting, locked the vehicle. He was unaccompanied. During the voyage, access to the garage deck was prohibited. A large sign on the bulkhead at the rear of the garage deck welcomed passengers on board Brittany Ferries ship MV Bretagne, stating it has the capacity to take 1,980 passengers and 580 vehicles.

It was late October, and the busy holiday season had concluded. The driver observed that the garage deck is less than half full of vehicles. Holding his backpack in his left hand, he followed the signs to the exit and climbed the stairs to Deck Seven. He entered the lounge area and made himself comfortable in a reclining seat, picking up a discarded Telegraph newspaper as he did so. For the next hour he continued to read the newspaper but made frequent discreet glances around the lounge area observing other passengers.

The man's UK passport gave his name as Paul Raymond Fisher, forty years of age. He was of slim build with a suntanned complexion. His unkempt, longish hair had been bleached by the sun and matched his thick untrimmed beard. He was casually dressed, wearing a well-worn Barbour jacket and jeans with military style tan desert boots which were similarly well-worn. Tied loosely around his neck he sported a cotton Shemagh scarf in an olive green and black coloured checkered pattern. His appearance was of a man who had spent the summer relaxing, travelling and enjoying the outdoor life.

Picking up his backpack he left the lounge area and took a slow deliberate stroll around the ship visiting the various decks and public areas as if looking for someone in particular. As midnight approached, he returned to the lounge area on Deck Seven. He occupied a reclining seat nearer to the all-night self-service restaurant. By now the more affluent travellers had taken to their night cabins.

Those remaining in the lounge, who had purchased a budget ticket without the luxury of a night cabin, were making themselves comfortable to spend the night on the reclining seats. Some tucked themselves into sleeping bags, whilst others just covered themselves with a jacket for added warmth. The lounge was to be Fisher's accommodation for the night.

By now the lounge lights have been dimmed creating a quiet, calm atmosphere. Some passengers slept or lay silently viewing the content on their iPads or iPhones. Fisher appeared restless. He strolled across to the self-service restaurant, selected a round of sandwiches and a mug of black coffee which he placed on a tray and paid for at the cash desk.

Exiting the self-service area, he stood for a moment looking around as if deciding where to sit before walking to a nearby table, which was already occupied by one man.

"Good morning, may I share your table?" asked Fisher in a polite manner.

The man looked up, nodded but did not speak. Fisher sat down opposite and continued: "Earlier this evening I noted you studying a map of London. Is that your destination?"

Again, the man just nodded but no words. Fisher pointed to the man's waxed canvas and leather back-pack, on the seat next to him. The front flap had an embroidered patch depicting the flag of Poland. "Are you Polish?"

This time the man made eye contact and spoke: "Yes, I am from Poland. I am visiting my Polish friends who work in London." He appeared willing to engage in further conversation.

He had the appearance of a man who had been trav-elling on the road for several days. His casual clothes, particularly his dirty, open-neck shirt, were crumpled and in need of a wash. He was about thirty-five years of age, of medium stature with a fit physique. A man who would handle himself well in a fight, thought Fisher.

Fisher held his hand out across the table.

"My name is Paul. I've just spent the summer bum-ming around Spain. Now it's back to England to find a job. I'm a qualified schoolteacher who decided to take a year's break from teaching to recharge my batteries."

The Polish man accepted the handshake, respond-ing with a firm grip.

"I am Aleksander. Aleksander Kozlowski and a plumber by trade. I am hoping to find work for the Winter in the UK and earn some good money to send back home to my family."

The two men continued talking and getting to know each other. They agreed to get some sleep on the reclining seats and then meet up again at 06:00 hours for an early breakfast before the ship docked at 07:45 hours. Fisher complimented Aleksander on his excellent command of the English language. He responded by explaining that whilst a student he spent several summer holidays touring the UK and was particularly fond of Scotland.

Over a cooked English breakfast Fisher explained that, for the next few days, he had arranged to stay at a friend's weekend cottage just a few miles from the port of Portsmouth in the small village of Bosham. He added that Aleksander was welcome to stay for a couple of days, which he gratefully accepted.

The ship docked on time. Together, in Fisher's Defender truck, the two men cleared Customs via the green 'Nothing to Declare' channel and began the onward journey to Bosham. The small, detached cottage was located in its own grounds, on the outskirts of Bosham village, in the pleasant rural West Sussex countryside.

During the journey there is little conversation between the two men. Fisher made several attempts to engage with Aleksander, pointing out places of interest, but received minimal response. The man seemed preoccupied with his own thoughts. Arriving at the cottage Fisher allocated Aleksander his own bedroom and pointed out the facilities. Although polite, the man remained reserved in his manner and showed little interest to engage in conversation.

Early morning on the second day of his stay, Aleksander was seen by Fisher standing at the far end of the back garden speaking on his mobile phone. On returning to the kitchen, he said he wished to visit a friend in London and would catch a train from the nearby railway station in Chichester. Fisher suggested they swap telephone numbers so they can keep in touch but, strangely, the offer was declined. Nevertheless, Fisher gave him a lift in his truck to the station.

Later the same evening, Aleksander returned to the cottage, having caught a taxi from Chichester Station. The two men sat in front of the wood burning open fire sharing a bottle of red wine, but there was not much conversation. Aleksander acknowledged he had met up with his friend in London but, strangely, was reluctant to talk about it. He was in a quiet reflective mood.

It was approaching midnight and the fire was burning itself out. Fisher decided it was time for bed. Aleksander had already indicated he would be departing in the morning to seek work in London.

Fisher's mobile iPhone unexpectedly rang which, at that late hour, took him by surprise. He took it from his breast shirt pocket, saying "Hello" and listened.

"Is this some kind of late-night joke?" He enquired speaking into the iPhone, with an element of annoyance, but continued to listen.

Suddenly the outside of the cottage, both back and front, was lit up by what appeared to be powerful searchlights.

"What the hell. It's the police. The cottage is surrounded. They say they're armed. We've got two minutes to leave the house with our hands over our heads."

Before Fisher had finished the sentence, Aleksander instinctively pulled a concealed handgun from inside his jacket and, in an aggressive stance, clasped the gun with both hands pointing it towards the front door. This was clearly not the reaction of a humble Polish plumber, but that of a well-trained professional military man. However, Fisher did not seem particularly surprised by this revelation.

Fisher immediately identified the weapon as a GSh-18 9mm semi-automatic pistol used by Russian elite special forces for close combat fighting. It was capable of holding an eighteen-round magazine with bullets that can pierce body armour. Similarly, this was not the knowledge you would expect from an ordinary schoolteacher! Life is full of surprises.

Fisher shouted to Aleksander.

"What the fuck are you doing. Keep holding that gun and they'll surely kill you."

He moved towards the nearby basket of logs and lifted a couple.

"Aleksander, quickly, hide your gun under these logs. He did what Fisher had directed.

Fisher opened the front door. With hands over their heads, they slowly and cautiously walked out into the glaring lights and stopped. From behind the glare of a searchlight, instructions were shouted for both men to lay prostrate on the ground with their hands spread out in front of them. This they did.

Several hooded and heavily armed individuals rushed forward. Without any degree of finesse, the two suspects were searched, rolled over and handcuffed. They were manhandled into a nearby van with blacked-out side and rear windows. The two remained guarded, and in silence, as other members of the arrest team searched the cottage.

The journey took about ninety minutes before the vehicle arrived at a gated and high security location. Once the vehicle had driven through the open gates it stopped and then reversed. Both men were roughly manhandled out of the vehicle and hurriedly taken into a custody suite complex. It appeared to be the rear entrance to a large, red, brick-built police station. Fisher assumed it was within the Metropolitan Police area but had no idea of the actual location.

Each prisoner was presented to the custody sergeant who was seated behind a large desk. One of the escorting team placed on the desk the passports of Fisher and Kozlowski. These had obviously been seized when the cottage had been searched. The custody sergeant examined each and compared the photographs with the two men. Without asking for confirmation, he entered the details onto a desktop computer.

In an adjoining room both men were photographed. Their fingerprints were taken, and DNA mouth swabs obtained. Throughout the process no words were exchanged or spoken by the arresting team of officers. Kozlowski was then taken away.

Fisher was placed into a small cell. The door was slammed shut and locked. He was in solitude staring at four blank walls. The handcuffs remained in place. Throughout, no explanation had been forthcoming. The only lighting was from a small, frosted window situated above the door which reflected light from the corridor. The furniture consisted of a wooden bed fixed to the floor with a basic, plastic-covered mattress to sleep on. No blankets were supplied. In the corner was located a stainless-steel toilet without a seat. The place was eerily quiet. There did not appear to be any other prisoners within the complex.

Fisher sat on the mattress, in silence and in near darkness, contemplating his fate. The cell was cold. After two hours the cell door was unlocked and opened. A large unsmiling figure of an overweight, middle-aged man stood in the doorway. With his right index finger, he gesticulated to Fisher to follow him into a nearby interview room.

He pointed to a chair chained to the floor: "Sit down."

In front of Fisher was a metal table secured to the floor. The man sat down in a chair opposite Fisher and placed a buff-coloured folder on the table. A younger man, possibly junior in rank, sat on a chair away from the table holding a notepad and pen.

"I'm detective sergeant Graham Moore, and you are in deep shit right up to your neck. So, if you want to see freedom anytime soon you'd better cooperate."

DS Moore was a man only two years away from retirement. He had spent much of his police career as a detective on the Robbery Squad dealing with some of the most violent and ruthless criminals in the UK. Perhaps the experience had helped contribute to his warped character. He saw bad and evil in everyone. His flushed patchy complexion indicated he was a man who regularly consumed alcohol to excess. A bitter and obnoxious man with few friends. Because of his frequent conflict with senior colleagues, he had recently been removed from his beloved Robbery Squad and temporarily assigned to divisional CID.

"Your friend has been identified as a Russian national sent to the UK on an assassination mission and you, my friend, are his little helper," said the detective with a large element of sarcasm.

Fisher responded. "I know nothing about that. I simply met him two days ago on the Saint-Malo to Portsmouth ferry and gave him accommodation. He said he was from Poland seeking work as a plumber in the UK. He was due to leave for London in the morning. I can't help you with any more information."

"Bullshit. You'll have to do better than that. Your likelihood of freedom is fast disappearing, and we'll throw away the key. One last chance to save your bacon."

Fisher remained calm. He was not going to be intimidated. He remained polite but positive with his reply:

"Sergeant Moore, you have not actually explained to me the reason for my arrest. In fact, you have not formally told me I have been arrested. Neither have you cautioned me, advised me of my rights to consult with a solicitor and, since I am being formally interviewed, why is this not being recorded on the tape machine sitting on this table?"

The sergeant's anger was clearly apparent in the reddening of his face.

"So, you think you know your rights. That suggests to me you have been in nick before. Have previous convictions, do you?"

Turning to his colleague he continued: "Constable, get me a cup of coffee and shut the door behind you."

Once the door was closed, the sergeant stood up and punched Fisher a heavy blow to the left side of his face. The force caused him to fall backwards with the chair hitting the ground. "That's my caution. You lump of shit."

Fisher remained on the ground, dazed by the force of the punch. His left cheek was red and swollen. He was still wearing the handcuffs and, thus, unable to defend himself. Further punches were delivered.

The sergeant's anger was still much in evidence. He grabbed Fisher by the scruff of his neck, pulled him to his feet and forcefully marched him back to the cell. Still holding him by the neck, he forced Fisher's head into the toilet bowl and flushed it. He then left the cell slamming the door behind him. Fisher staggered to his feet, dripping wet, to lay on the mattress. He spent the night cold, wet and alone.

Early next morning he was taken from his cell to the reception area where Kozlowski was already standing by the custody sergeant's desk. On seeing the swelling of Fisher's left cheek, and still wet hair, he was about to ask what had happened. Fisher shook his head and mouthed "No."

The custody sergeant explained that both men are being remanded in custody pending further police investigation. Having been arrested under the Terrorism Act they can be held for up to fourteen days without charge. They were to be sent to separate detention centres. Each was then escorted from the complex.

CHAPTER TWO

The Review

The Security Service (MI5) is the United King-
dom's domestic counter-intelligence and security
agency, directed to protect British parliamentary
democracy and interests. It deals with coun-
ter-terrorism and espionage within the UK and is
responsible to the Secretary of State for the Home
Office. The Secret Intelligence Service (MI6) is the
foreign intelligence service of the United King-
dom, tasked mainly with covert overseas oper-
ations in the collection and analysis of human
intelligence. The agency is directly accountable to
the Secretary of State for Foreign and Common-
wealth Affairs.

It was now a week on from the arrest and detention of
Fisher and Kozlowski. British Intelligence had been

busy undertaking much research and investigation into the case.

Friday afternoon, at 14:00 hours, an intelligence debrief was convened in the regal splendour of a secure conference room within the confines of Whitehall. Representatives attended from the intelligence agencies (MI5 and MI6), the Military, the Police (including detective sergeant Graham Moore), the Home Office and the Foreign and Commonwealth Office.

With all representatives seated around the circular conference table, and the meeting about to commence, a lone man quietly entered the room by a side door. He sat in a chair away from the rest of the group and with a discreet nod acknowledged the Chair. He observed the proceedings and took notes, writing in a leather-bound notebook balanced on his knee, but did not actively participate. He was slim, clean shaven and smartly dressed in a well-tailored navy-blue pinstripe suit: displaying the confidence of a professional man at ease in these surroundings.

The Chair was from MI5. In accordance with protocol for such intelligence meetings, the representatives acknowledged the agencies they represent but were not asked to publicly introduce themselves by name. The content of the meeting was classified as Secret and the Minutes would be recorded as such.

The Chair updated the meeting on the details and outcome of Operation Backfire: Some months earlier sensitive intelligence sources had intercepted communications emanating from abroad regarding an operation to assassinate a Russian oligarch billionaire resident in London. His activities had apparently displeased his previous associates. The name of the oligarch was yet to be identified, as was the location, date and method of assassination. British Intelligence had commenced Operation Backfire to identify the participants and thwart the assassination attempt.

Before the man calling himself, Aleksander Kozlowski had entered the UK, he was the subject of surveillance by British intelligence agencies. This included when he visited London to meet up with a second member of the proposed assassination team. At that time, the identity of the second man was not known. Both men had now been identified as Russian nationals and members of an elite special forces team.

The 'London' man had recently been under limited surveillance. The fast-moving pace of events had made it impossible to deploy a full surveillance team in time. Only two team members had been available. Unfortunately, he was able to evade being followed. He had disappeared and was now back in Russia. No doubt, he had returned to his home base with the message that the intended assassination mission had been identified and disrupted. His 'masters' would not know the fate of their operative using the alias Aleksander Kozlowski.

The Chair reported that Aleksander Kozlowski remained in detention with his case signed over to MI5 for further action. No public announcement would be released on his detention or future.

The potential target for the assassination attempt had now been visited by Special Branch, briefed on the circumstances and advised on his future security needs.

All actions had been approved at the highest government level.

Working with other friendly intelligence agencies within Europe, British Intelligence had that morning established that in recent years both men had covertly, and using false identities, operated in Berlin, Stockholm and other countries during periods which coincided with suspicious deaths, usually by poisoning, of former Russian nationals. The information remained vague and lacked detail or the necessary corroboration. Further development was required.

As the Chair began her closing comments, the man sitting alone walked across the room to a side table containing refreshments and poured himself a cup of black coffee. He stood by the refreshment table drinking his coffee and listening to the Chair conclude the meeting. DS Moore turned in his seat and made eye contact with the man, showing a glance of recognition.

Being inquisitive, DS Moore joined the man at the refreshment table and in a quiet voice asked: "Have we met before?"

He glanced at the purple Whitehall visitor's pass attached to the man's breast pocket: it was devoid of a name.

"I'm Julian Lawson, a senior member of the Security Service better known as MI5." He looked at Moore in a knowing, defiant almost intimidating manner, but said nothing further.

Moore still couldn't recall where they had met before. As he stood thinking, an uncomfortable nervous feeling began to run through his body. Was it recently, and possibly, under different circumstances?

Lawson placed his coffee cup on the table and turned to face Moore. He spoke slowly and deliberately:

"Detective sergeant Graham Moore, one word from me to the appropriate authorities and you will lose your freedom, lose your career and lose your handsome police pension."

He paused, looked directly into Moore's eyes and continued:

"To paraphrase you, detective sergeant Graham Moore, you could be in deep shit. Good day officer."

With that, Lawson left the conference room and exited the building, handing his visitor's pass in at Reception.

Standing on the steps of the building he contemplated his next move. Lawson still felt a sense of anger about the thuggish DS Moore and decided not to return directly to MI5 HQ. He turned left and slowly strolled up Whitehall towards Trafalgar Square. He enjoyed walking in Central London; Westminster in particular, with its history and grand buildings. It was now early November; the hordes of tourists had dissipated and there was an autumn crispness in the calm afternoon air.

He glanced to his right looking up at the impressive tall war memorial, The Cenotaph, built in Portland stone and the site of the National Service of Remembrance. To his left was Downing Street, offices of the Prime Minister and Chancellor of the Exchequer; the entrance protected by tall black steel double gates, which are closed, and with staff entering the street via a side security-controlled checkpoint. The site is protected by armed police from the Diplomatic Protection Group.

Lawson continued his walk, passing the Cabinet Office and admiring the grandeur of the buildings in Whitehall, which is recognised as the centre of the Government of the United Kingdom.

After a short distance he stopped, stepped to the outside of the pavement and looked across the road at Banqueting House: the only remaining component of the Palace of Whitehall, the residence of English Monarchs from 1530 to 1698. He took out his iPhone and photographs the building. It brought back happy memories of times spent with his late wife. The spectacular venue had hosted feasts and celebrations for almost four hundred years.

Several years back, with his wife, in evening dress they had attended a lavish Christmas Dinner in the Main Hall with its soaring neo-classic columns and magnificent Rubens painted ceilings. They had attended as guests of a military regiment. Their weekend was spent at the nearby Royal Horseguards Hotel. A very precious time.

Lawson continued walking towards Trafalgar Square, turned left onto The Mall, and passed under Admiralty Arch and on into St James's Park. He purchased a glass of beer at the open-air restaurant and sat down at a table away from the other customers. It was time to reflect.

Operation Backfire had taken over his life full-time for the past few months. Having taken on the cover identity of Paul Fisher he had travelled to Spain in his Land Rover Defender truck to spend the Summer developing his background story posing as a schoolteacher, taking a year's sabbatical, and being an enthusiastic amateur photographer.

A second element of the operation was to use the opportunity to gather intelligence and take photographs for the UK National Crime Agency, on the illicit activities of known British criminals living in Spain and involved with large scale international drug trafficking.

Operation Backfire had not gone entirely according to plan. No operation ever does. All such operations require quick decision making, with alternative strategies constantly under review, and the ability to redeploy at a moment's notice. The original intention had been to develop a longer relationship with the target Aleksander Kozlowski to, hopefully, meet his London friend and gain a greater knowledge of their plans and contacts.

However, when Aleksander travelled to London on the second day of being in England and met up with his 'friend' the UK surveillance team established the assassination of their target was planned for the next day. It was to be a close contact shooting when the target, a Russian oligarch, was visiting horse racing stables in Norfolk to view his latest acquisition. Aleksander's friend had detailed plans of the stables, plus coloured high-definition aerial photographs of the establishment and surrounding area.

Two days earlier, it had now been established, the 'London' man had visited the horse racing stables and undertaken a detailed recognisance of the area. On that occasion he had parked a white Ford Transit van in the nearby railway station car park and caught a train back to London. It remained there overnight, along with other parked vehicles, and did not look out of place.

Subsequently, access had been gained, by MI5 personnel, to the rear of the van. It contained two trail motorcycles with the necessary crash helmets and leather protective clothing, evidently for use in their getaway following the assassination. Enquiries identified the van had been hired from a company in East London, using false documents. The two men had intended to escape the UK using the services of a rogue pilot from a small private airfield in the southeast of England.

Assassination by shooting was not a subtle way to dispose of an individual. This public and obvious execution was deliberate. The oligarch had displeased certain people in authority and death was his punishment. This was intended to send a clear message to others considering such disloyalty that they should take note. The two assassins had arranged to be spirited out of the UK immediately after the killing.

Having gained this intelligence, from the surveillance undertaken on the two men, the UK agencies needed to act without delay. The evening raid to detain Kozlowski along with Lawson, in his cover identity of Fisher, was initiated. The arrest of Lawson had not been part of the original operation, and he had not been forewarned it was about to happen. Lawson was an experienced officer who knew the rules of the game. To have disclosed his identity, as an MI5 officer, at the time of their arrest and initial detention would have jeopardised the operation. So, he played along as the innocent Paul Fisher. However, next morning when Kozlowski was remanded in custody, Lawson was secretly 'spirited away' and collected by an MI5 colleague. Detective sergeant Graham Moore was not made aware of Lawson's true role until their encounter at the Whitehall intelligence debrief.

Prior to 1991, the former Soviet Union had been made up of fifteen republics: Russia being the largest, and most dominant, with a population of one hundred and forty-six million. Economic and internal political turmoil contributed to its eventual disintegration.

The failing Soviet state was in chaos. This allowed informal deals with former USSR officials, mostly in Russia and Ukraine to acquire state property very cheaply, or sometimes at no cost. Some individuals achieved vast wealth quickly. Post-Soviet oligarchs were often related or close associates of government officials. Criminal bosses were often connected to the Russian government. Billions of dollars were secretly transferred to private Swiss bank accounts. Oligarchs became extremely unpopular.

In 2006 Russia passed a law giving its security agents licence to track down and kill enemies of the state living abroad. Oligarchs considered to have acted against the interests of Russia, are legitimate targets for assassination. They are regarded as traitors.

Julian Lawson was now in his third year with MI5. Like all MI5 officers, this was his cover name. He operated using a completely false identity. His work was secretive and often dangerous. For this reason, details of his home address, telephone number and car registration were 'blocked' from public scrutiny. Any individual or company applying to the Driver & Vehicle Licensing Agency for information would receive a 'no information available' response, and Lawson would discreetly be notified of the enquiry. He depended on the trust and professionalism of his colleagues, yet he doesn't know their true identities and they don't know his; a strange world he still found difficult to accept. Now, in recent months, he had operated using a third different identity as Paul Fisher.

He was born Benjamin Swan and had joined the Police as a young and ambitious uniformed constable. Early in his career he had been appointed a detective constable in the CID. Life was good and exciting. He enjoyed the freedom that came with the role. What young man would not enjoy being trained to drive high powered police cars on pursuit and surveillance driving courses or trained in the use of firearms and being involved on operations with the military. Being young, and now looking back with hindsight, he did not initially appreciate the responsibilities and dangers that came with the role.

Life was good and would go on forever. He had a beautiful wife, who was a schoolteacher, and they had plans for a lifetime. They had met while students together at Canterbury Christ Church University, where he had obtained a degree in Politics and Law. They had been married for ten years when unexpectedly, she was taken ill. Extremely ill with terminal cancer. The end came quickly. She was always in his thoughts, but he rarely spoke about her.

By now, Ben was a detective chief inspector attached to the Counter-Terrorism Directorate operating in the UK and Ireland. In Ireland, driving to an intelligence conference, the police car he was in was ambushed. One officer was seriously injured. Ben shot and killed the armed attacker. A subsequent court ruled his action was justified. Nevertheless, in the eyes of the paramilitary organisation involved they would continue to identify him as a legitimate target for revenge.

He had been impressed by the natural beauty of Ireland. He particularly enjoyed a visit he had made to the West Coast of County Galway, part of the Wild Atlantic Way and one of the most beautiful places in Europe. He was saddened by the sectarianism and hatred he had witnessed during his time working in Ireland. It was unlikely it would now be safe for him to return there.

Shortly after the shooting incident in Ireland, Ben Swan was recruited to operate as a full member of the Security Service, MI5. It was an initial two-year attachment with his police rank suspended for the duration. His new cover identity was as Julian Lawson. Recently, he had accepted the invitation to extend his involvement with MI5 for a further two-year deployment.

For Lawson, Operation Backfire is still an active operation for MI5. The man, Aleksander Kozlowski, is still in detention. Lawson has been assigned to undertake the appropriate interrogations. Lawson feels no animosity towards him. Yes, he is a trained assassin, but he is employed to protect the society he believes in. No doubt, he considers himself the good guy seeking out and destroying the enemy.

Lawson thought back to his own experience in Ireland. He had shot and killed a 'terrorist' who had tried to kill him. He recalled pulling off the balaclava of the dead terrorist and feeling sad that he was a teenager but, at the same time, knowing the killing was justified. Lawson wondered if the young man had embarked on his mission believing he was the good guy attacking the enemy.

Lawson's opinion of DS Moore was different. He recalled the oath he had taken when he joined the Police: *"I do solemnly and sincerely declare and affirm that I will well and truly serve the Queen in the office of constable, with fairness, integrity, diligence and impartiality, upholding fundamental human rights and according equal respect to all people: and that I will, to the best of my power, cause the peace to be kept."*

Throughout his career Lawson had endeavoured to uphold the values of honesty, fairness, impartiality and respect for all. He had been proud to be a police officer. For the first time in his life, he had been on the receiving end of police brutality. The trust and values he held dear had been trashed.

Earlier in the week, Lawson had researched the background of DS Moore. He had been a bright ambitious recruit and a first-rate rugby player. Being identified as a 'good thief catcher' saw him appointed to the Robbery Squad. Working long hours and the demands of the job caused his marriage to breakdown. An acrimonious divorce followed. Like many of his colleagues, Moore now lived alone and drank too much. Throughout most of his career in the Robbery Squad he had daily dealt with violent ruthless villains with no respect for the normal standards of morality. Nevertheless, Lawson felt ashamed and angry that Moore belonged to the organisation of which he was proud to be a part.

It was time to get back to the office. He checked his watch: it was nearly 16:00 hours. He left the quietness of St James's Park and commenced the ten-minute walk back to Thames House, MI5 HQ. He crossed onto Horse Guards Road and along Parliament Square, passing The Palace of Westminster and along Millbank, entering the main entrance of Thames House. The imposing Portland stone and granite eight storey Neoclassical building is located on the north bank of the River Thames. Being the HQ of the UK Security Service, there is no signage on the outside of the building to identify its function.

Lawson stopped at ground floor Reception and clipped to his breast pocket his security pass. It displays his colour photograph and incorporates proximity-card technology giving access to secure areas in the building without the need to physically use a swipe card. The system also records arrival and departure times of the holder. He then walked through the airport style full-body scanner, which was also able to detect non-metal objects, and into the main part of the building. Staff are only permitted to take previously approved, and examined, electronic items into the building. All visitors must leave electronic items, including iPads, iPhones and cameras at Reception and at all times be accompanied by an authorised member of staff.

Each floor of the eight-storey building is occupied by a different department within the organisation. Security is paramount. The handling and movement of sensitive and secret intelligence is scrupulously managed. Doors remain locked until access is required. Access to each level, and each individual section, is strictly limited to authorised personnel who have an operational requirement to be there. Entry to each secure area is by use of the person's security pass. Entry and departure times are recorded at each of the Security points. Staff are not permitted to visit another section or department without a specific work-related reason.

Director Jane Rigby was in her office and warmly welcomed the return of Julian Lawson. It was their first meeting since he returned to the UK from Operation Backfire. Jane had been his immediate boss since he joined MI5. She is an extremely knowledgeable and competent operations director, who possesses a genuine care for the welfare of her team.

In accordance with strict Security Service policy, all personnel operate using a cover identity. Neither their true identity, nor personal background, is known to their work colleagues. Lawson assessed Jane was in her mid-forties, had received a public-school education with a middle upper class family background. She is slim, has a confident, calm self-assured manner and is elegant in her style of dress with well-manicured fingernails. Jane wears tortoise-shell frame reading spectacles, usually positioned around her neck on a thin gold chain.

When Jane's generation joined the Security Service it was through a secret process of being identified as a potential candidate and then recruited. It was by invitation only: one could not apply to join. Most recruits had received a university education from either Oxford or Cambridge and with a family member holding a senior position within government or the military. In recent years, the pool for potential recruits had widened with individuals now able to apply.

She had read Julian's classified report on Operation Backfire, including the details of his unexpected 'detention' and the brutal treatment carried out by the police officer, DS Graham Moore. Jane was pleased the assassination attempt had been thwarted but expressed concern about Julian's health. He assured her he was well.

"Do you wish to make a formal complaint and have Moore's conduct investigated?" she asked.

"No. I spoke with him this afternoon at the intelligence briefing and left him in no doubt his card had been marked. He now knows he is responsible for unlawfully assaulting a senior MI5 officer. He doesn't know my police identity. I feel ashamed he is a serving police officer and determined to see he doesn't bring further discredit to the service."

"I'll have a confidential word with the Commissioner to ensure Moore is moved to a non-operational role with his retirement brought forward," replied Jane.

Jane gave Lawson an update on Operation Backfire and on the decision-making process the department had undertaken. Following the detention of Aleksander Kozlowski, and his subsequent transfer to Belmarsh top security prison, the initial consideration had been to keep up Lawson's cover as Paul Fisher and integrate him into the prison system to join up with Kozlowski, the rationale being that Kozlowski, back at the cottage, had been given assistance from 'Fisher' to hide his gun and then at the custody suite had witnessed that he had been beaten. Therefore, it was suggested putting the two together in the prison environment might coax more information from Kozlowski. However, when the full debrief was forthcoming from the surveillance team it was established that the intelligence they had gained was valued at 'gold' and sufficient to establish and prove beyond doubt their intention to assassinate the identified Russian oligarch.

This was a fast-moving investigation. MI5 had now ascertained the identity of the target. He was very security conscious and whenever he left his gated Chelsea mansion, he would wear a bulletproof vest and be accompanied by two armed bodyguards, who had previously been members of the elite Russia Spetsnaz army group. The Kozlowski assassination mission had included a detailed and credible plan to also disable, and kill, if necessary, the two-armed bodyguards.

Kozlowski's gun, now recovered from the cottage in Bosham, was a 9mm semi-automatic GSh-18 favoured by Russian special forces. It had since been the subject of forensic examination and confirmed the 18 round magazine contained bullets designed to pierce body armour.

Jane confirmed that Kozlowski was classified as a high-risk terrorist and, as such, would be kept in isolation and not permitted to mix with other prisoners, the exception being mealtimes and the one hour a day exercise period, when he would share the time with one other 'terrorist' prisoner being detained under the same restrictions.

Lawson commented, "Is that not dangerous?"

"Not in the slightest." Jane allowed herself a mild smile: "He's one of our best agents."

They then discussed the next phase of Operation Backfire with Julian's involvement in the interrogation of the man Aleksander Kozlowski. In accordance with MI5 policy the aim would be to 'turn him' to cooperate and give them detailed background information on the organisation he was from. Gaining intelligence on their adversaries is the principal goal of the Security Service. Prosecution is at the bottom of the list of priorities.

Lawson asked if the 'sponsors' of the planned assassination had been identified. Was it on the orders of a criminal organisation or authorised by government?

Jane replied, that in the current climate they often merged, and it was difficult to differentiate between the two. The consensus of opinion favoured state involvement.

Jane suggested that Julian take a couple of days rest away from operational duties before embarking on the interrogation of Kozlowski. He was safely detained at HM Prison Belmarsh, a Category-A men's prison, located in south-east London. The prison was particularly for those concerning matters of national security.

CHAPTER THREE

Home to Petworth

Several years before the unexpected death of his young wife they had invested in their future by buying a Victorian detached cottage, with twenty-two acres of woodland, on the outskirts of the rural county town of Petworth in West Sussex, which is located within the South Downs National Park.

The historic small town of Petworth has a population of about three thousand inhabitants and is mentioned in the Domesday Book of 1086 as having forty-four households, eleven smallholders and nine slaves. The large seventeenth century stately Petworth House, with its seven-hundred-acre deer park, dominates the town. The entire estate is enclosed behind a thick high wall, some five miles in circumference. The main imposing gatehouse faces the main road running through the town.

The cottage remained Lawson's home and retreat. He lived there alone, but due to Operation Backfire and his time in Spain he had not been home since the summer. Mr and Mrs Graysmark, an elderly retired couple who live nearby, visit the cottage twice a week to undertake housekeeping and care for the garden. The Petworth Estate is now owned and managed by the National Trust. When working in London, particularly if it had been a long day, Julian would use the staff overnight quarters located within the large complex of Thames House (MI5 HQ).

During his unexpected detention, members of the MI5 team had discreetly taken possession of his Land Rover Defender truck, from where he had left it in Bosham, and parked it in their Thames House secure underground garage. Much to his pleasant surprise, it had been valeted and awaited his collection. He had never seen it looking so clean.

It was early evening when he drove out of the City and began the fifty-five-mile journey to Petworth. During the journey he mentally switched in his mind that he was 'off duty' for the weekend and, thus, in true identity mode as Ben Swan. He had spent the Summer as Paul Fisher, then a couple of days ago switched back to being Julian Lawson. Now, for the weekend he would be Ben Swan. On Monday, catching the train to London he would switch back to being Julian Lawson, MI5 officer. He smiled inwardly and hoped no more changes of identity were in the pipeline!

On reaching Petworth town he parked outside the late-night general store to purchase, using cash, some basic food for the weekend from the assistant Brenda, who welcomed him as 'Ben'. To the locals he was still known as Ben Swan. He had never disclosed to them that he was a police officer. Being identified as a police officer with the Counter-Terrorism Directorate, working in Ireland, brought with it obvious dangers.

When asked about his occupation, he would simply say he was a self-employed consultant who often worked away from home: a boring job that paid the mortgage. That usually stopped further inquisitive questions being asked. He explained his recent absence by telling Brenda he had been working in Europe for the summer. She certainly didn't know that for the past three years he had operated as a member of MI5.

Arriving at his cottage he went through his usual routine of placing his 'MI5 Julian Lawson' identification documents in the study wall safe and taking out his own 'Ben Swan' driving licence and bank cards. He noted his Glock 19 handgun, in its brown leather holder, taking up the rear section of the safe, next to which sat a magazine containing fifteen rounds (bullets) of ammunition.

The sight of the gun brought back vivid memories of his time in Ireland and his shooting of the paramilitary youth who had ambushed and tried to kill him. Although he had been a police-trained and authorised firearms user for many years, it was the first occasion he had fired a gun in an operational situation, and that had resulted in the killing of a fellow human being. His actions had been ruled justified, in a court of law, but he continued to feel much inner sadness.

The killing had made him a likely target for a revenge attack on his life. Therefore, he had been given written authority to carry a concealed gun in the UK when on or off duty. He had chosen not to carry it unless he was made aware of a specific threat. Until that occurred, the gun would remain securely locked in his home wall safe.

He had a hot shower, made himself a cheese and pickle sandwich, his favourite reserve snack, as he was not in the mood to cook a meal. He then poured out a large tumbler of malt whisky and relaxed in his favoured leather reclining chair whilst listening to an Andrea Bocelli CD. He was home and it felt good. Several more whiskies followed.

He woke early the following morning with a hangover, still in his reclining chair. He did not now feel so good. In recent months, he had experienced some strange and disturbing dreams. In last evening's dream a child was drowning, and, despite his desperate efforts, he had been unable to save her. Similar dreams had him in situations where violence was being perpetrated against another individual and he had been unable to help them. Perhaps, it was a subconscious reflection of his lifestyle and recent events.

He checked his watch: it was 06:30 hours. Slowly leaning forward and getting to his feet, he stood upright and shook his head in an attempt to clear his thoughts. He walked through to the kitchen, flicked on the coffee machine and stood waiting. After a couple of minutes, he poured himself a mug of steaming hot, black coffee, unlocked the external door, walked out into the rear garden and sat down on the wooden bench.

The cottage backs on to his twenty-two-acre woodland. It is divided into three distinct areas of trees, consisting of Sweet Chestnut, Beech and Scots Pine. A log cabin is located in the centre of the Beech tree wood. He hadn't visited it for several months, so he thought it an ideal opportunity to take a walk down the winding woodland track to tidy up the cabin. No doubt, the outside area would be covered with fallen leaves and the vegetation overgrown. Another pleasant surprise greeted him. It was evident Mr Graysmark had recently visited the cabin and tided up. He had also chopped and stacked a fresh supply of logs. There was no work for Ben to do, so he made himself comfortable on the outside wooden bench and relaxed.

Back in the cottage he had a shower and a shave and got dressed into a fresh set of casual clothes. Mrs Graysmark had obviously visited in recent days: the house was spotlessly clean and smelled of fresh lavender polish. He thought he must thank both Mr and Mrs Graysmark for their efforts before he returned to London on Monday.

Following several more cups of black coffee, he telephoned Mr and Mrs Graysmark to let them know he was back and to thank them for what they had done. They were pleased to hear he was safely back home and invited him to their house for a midday lunch, which he accepted.

Mr and Mrs Graysmark reside in one of several rented cottages located within the Petworth Park estate. Ben had been given to understand that at one time both had worked for the estate. Embarrassingly, he did not know their Christian names. They had become his part-time housekeeper and gardener following the death of his wife, having been recommended by Brenda from the general store in the High Street.

To reach their cottage Ben, driving his Defender truck, entered the Petworth Park Estate and drove slowly along the private road cutting through the park to enjoy the view of the grazing Fallow deer, said to be over seven-hundred in number and the largest herd in the UK. From the outside, Petworth House is somewhat obscured behind the surrounding high walls. Driving through the park was his first opportunity to take in the full magnificence of Petworth House and its Late Baroque architecture.

Mr and Mrs Graysmark were in their front garden waiting to greet him with their large old English sheep dog, Molly. Ben was very fond of Molly and, when spending a leisurely weekend in his woodland, he would often 'borrow' her for company. She actually had her own dog's basket in his cabin.

Mrs Graysmark had prepared a full roast beef lunch with potatoes cooked in duck fat. She suggested Ben had lost weight during his time in Spain and needed a good meal. It was a very tasty lunch, and he was not about to argue with her assessment. As a thank you, he gave them a box of Belgium chocolates he had purchased at the duty-free shop on the ferry.

After lunch they relaxed in the sitting room with Mr Graysmark serving brandy. During the course of the lunch, Ben discreetly noted Mr and Mrs Graysmark referring to each other by their Christian names: Christopher and Helen. He assessed they were in their early eighties. They were excellent company and, despite their age, appeared knowledgeable and up-to-date on current affairs. During the course of the meal Ben ascertained that they did not have children.

In addition to his brandy, Christopher lit up a large Cuban cigar, commenting it was one of the luxuries he still enjoyed from the time when they lived abroad. In response to Ben asking, Christopher said that much of their working life had been spent living and working in a variety of foreign countries on behalf of 'Her Majesty's Government.' Ben was intrigued by the formality of his words. Christopher continued to explain that it was only after he retired, and they returned to the UK but owned no property that they rented their current cottage, embarking on casual part-time employment with the Petworth Park Estate.

Helen interrupted the conversation.

"Tell us about yourself. We know your wife sadly died about three years ago but further than that, and the fact that you travel, we know extraordinarily little about you."

Ben gave his stock reply that he had a boring job as a consultant, adding:

"It's in management. I arrive at a company, look at their systems, give advice and then move on. There's nothing further to add. All quite boring."

Christopher commented:

"Helen says you're the tidiest person she's ever met. Everything in your cottage is in perfect alignment, with nothing out of place, and there are no photographs or items of memorabilia to suggest your interests or hobbies."

Helen interjected:

"Please Ben, we don't mean that to sound rude. We know you're passionate about your woodland, but I just mentioned to Christopher about the absence of photographs and memorabilia."

Ben smiled but said nothing and continued enjoying his glass of brandy. He had earlier declined Christopher's offer of a cigar.

In response to Helen's observation about his cottage, Ben took the opportunity to, once again, thank both for their work in caring for his house and garden. This led on to Christopher and Helen talking about their enjoyment in continuing to work, and be useful, in their old age.

Christopher commented: "When you get to our age you become invisible. People regard you as useless and boring."

Helen added with a smile: "Nobody looks at you twice. The only adverts on TV for the over sixties are planning for death or extreme old age or illness."

Christopher added: "You don't stop dreaming, you don't stop wishing and you don't stop living just because you're old."

After a pause he continued: "And you don't stop observing and assessing things and people around you."

With a sense of mischief Ben joined the conversation:

"Goodness me, this is getting very philosophical for a cosy Saturday afternoon."

He paused and then continued:

"My turn to make an observation on the comment you made about working for Her Majesty's Government. No doubt, that was with the Foreign and Commonwealth Office. Which department?"

Christopher didn't answer but turned to Helen as if seeking reassurance. Both then smiled.

Ben continued with his mischievous questioning:

"I bet in your day the location of your HQ was unknown. Not like today: the birthday cake style monstrosity of a building which sits on the banks of the River Thames at Vauxhall."

Christopher replied: "I couldn't possibly comment."

Ben added: "And noticing some of the American memorabilia on your sideboard, I would take a guess that one of your more enjoyable postings was to the British Embassy in Washington."

Christopher, continuing with the banter, responded:

"And my thoughts about your occupation. A very non-committal young man. Not the sort to be doing a boring job. When I first came to work for you, I recall arriving at your cottage early one morning and seeing you with a mirror on a stick thingy examining the underside of your truck. I thought to myself: I don't think he's checking for rust!"

He paused, gave a knowing smile, and said: "Let's have another brandy."

Ben responded: "Like you, I couldn't possibly comment. I've enjoyed my visit and your company. Yes please, I would like another brandy."

He thought to himself: wily old fox.

It had been an interesting and worthwhile visit for Ben. Prior to the visit he had regarded Christopher and Helen as just a pleasant elderly couple who were eking out their pensions by doing part-time domestic work. He was embarrassed to feel he had not looked beyond that stereotype. It was now evident that in his prime Christopher had been a senior officer within MI6: only senior grades take up a posting at the British Embassy in Washington.

Having consumed several glasses of brandy, Ben decided he should leave his truck parked outside Christopher and Helen's cottage and walk the two miles back to his home. It is late afternoon and lightly raining: the sort of fresh Autumn weather he enjoyed being out in.

He collected his Barbour jacket from his truck and began an invigorating walk through the seven-hundred-acre deer park, taking the route alongside the serpentine lake. The magnificent landscape was the work of Lancelot Capability Brown, undertaken at great expense in the seventeen-fifties. In his day, the famous artist JMW Turner had been a frequent guest at Petworth House and often painted landscape views of the park. Many of his works are on display in the house.

Back at home, Ben decided to have an early night.

Sunday morning, he was awake by 06:00 hours and feeling restless. He made himself a light breakfast of toast and black coffee while he considered his plans for the day, which would include collecting his Defender truck.

Walking back through Petworth Deer Park to collect his truck, he watched groups of National Trust members, mainly families, enjoying the quiet peace and freedom of the countryside. He had a sense of personal isolation and, in his mind, began to compare his life-style as a police officer and now as an MI5 officer.

The police service is, in many respects, a family. Camaraderie is one of its strengths. Police officers form close working and social relationships, and know each other's history: their previous deployments, families and hobbies. When transferred to a different department, friendships often continue. Colleagues will always help or support each other in time of need.

As a police officer, at a loose end on a Sunday morning, Ben would have phoned a police friend and invited him out for a lunchtime drink. For obvious and practical reasons, since being in MI5, he now had infrequent contact with his former colleagues.

Being a member of MI5 is totally different. It is a secret organisation. Personnel operate under false identities. Strict policy prevents disclosing true identities or information about their background or family. Social contact outside of the working environment is frowned upon. Disclosure of an agent's identity to the Media or an 'enemy' intelligence organisation would severely limit an officer's advancement. Ben recalled one of his colleagues, who had recently given evidence at the Old Bailey Law Courts behind a screen and only identified by a single letter, commenting on his life in MI5 as: "I am always present, but never there."

Chapter Four

Operation Backfire

06:00 hours Monday morning, and Ben prepared to leave his Petworth home for London. The routine included returning his own Ben Swan documents to his wall safe and taking out the documents with his cover identity. The moment he secured the safe locked, he was Julian Lawson.

At 08:30 hours Julian Lawson arrived at MI5 HQ and walks to his office. A number was displayed on the door, but no name. As with all offices within the building, when not occupied it is a strict requirement that it be locked. Another requirement is that no photographs or other personal items are permitted to be on display. The room was sterile of personality, deliberately so, with nothing to identify the current occupant. As he entered his office he was reminded of Mr and Mrs Graysmark's observations of yesterday regarding his 'tidy' cottage.

At 09:00 hours he attended the conference Silver Room on the seventh floor and was joined by his colleague Mark Holloway. They had worked together on several cases. Mark was of a similar age to Julian. He was about six feet two inches in height, slim build with short cut thick black hair. He possessed a good sense of humour, with a ready smile, and a confident manner. As with other members of the organisation, Julian did not know his true identity or background. They were now to be involved in the interrogation of the detained man Aleksander Kozlowski.

Shortly after, Director Jane Rigby joined the two men in the conference Silver Room and brought with her Claire, an MI5 senior intelligence analyst. The purpose of the meeting was to discuss Operation Backfire and the forthcoming interrogation of the man, Aleksander Kozlowski.

The basic rules of engagement had already been set out. At senior government level it had previously been agreed that Kozlowski would be given the opportunity to cooperate. This would involve admitting his involvement in the assassination attempt, fully disclosing his past activities and identifying details of the organisation to which he belonged. In exchange he would not face prosecution. His reward would, possibly, be to be placed on the 'rehabilitation programme' and given a new identity, together with a pension.

Having opened the meeting Jane asked Claire to present the report on the current available intelligence. Claire gave an update on the second target, previously referred to as the 'London friend.' He had travelled to the UK using a false Polish passport in the name Jakub Wozniak. He arrived two weeks prior to the planned assassination attempt, initially staying at a Travel Lodge hotel near London Heathrow Airport.

After a week he had travelled to Peterborough, a city seventy-six miles north of London, and booked into a three-star hotel. He told hotel staff members he was on holiday and had an interest in racehorses. The staff had been interviewed and were able to assist the investigation as to his movements. The forensic team had obtained from the hotel in Peterborough Wozniak's DNA, fingerprint impressions and photographs from the internal CCTV.

He went out most days from the hotel to visit the local horse racing stables. He would arrive at the stables with his camera, and a racing newspaper under his arm, and mix with other 'punters' to watch the horses working out on the gallops and later being groomed in the yard. This was a common occurrence, and he didn't stand out.

After about a week, early in the morning, he departed from the hotel, telling staff he needed to be back in London. That was the day he met up with Aleksander Kozlowski. The meeting was monitored by the MI5 surveillance team. It was established that the two men intended to carry out the assassination the following day when their target, the Russian oligarch, was scheduled to visit the racing stables in Norfolk.

Later the same evening Wozniak had returned to his hotel in Peterborough. This course of action had split the capability of the surveillance team. Only two members were available to be deployed to follow him on his return journey to Peterborough.

That evening, at a top-level meeting at MI5 HQ, the decision was taken to disrupt the operation.

Unfortunately, the surveillance-conscious Jakub Wozniak had sensed he was under surveillance. He aborted his mission and made a hurried escape, catching a train to Birmingham Airport and then an Aeroflot flight to Minsk, the capital of Belarus.

Director Jane Rigby added that on arriving at Minsk Airport he travelled directly to the Military Security Service HQ in the city centre.

"How do we know that?" enquired Lawson.

Rigby responded:

"When he returned to the hotel in Peterborough, and whilst he went to the restaurant for a meal, a member of our team covertly gained access to his room. In the lining of his shoulder bag, she inserted a miniature tracking device. This enabled us to monitor his movements when he arrived back in Belarus."

After a pause she continued:

"Shortly after his arrival at the Security Service HQ, the transmissions abruptly ceased. No doubt, our device was found during their own technical security checks. From our point of view, this is a useful result. His visit direct to Security Service HQ adds further confirmation that the two men are still on the payroll of the military. It has also sent a clear message that UK Intelligence had detected their plans to undertake an assassination."

Rigby then commented:

"All subjects, along with their personal property, when detained by this agency, undergo a full electronic body scan to ensure they are not carrying or are fitted with a tracking device. Kozlowski was checked when detained and was negative."

She also confirmed his mobile telephone had been examined with a negative result. It was a cheap pay-as-you-go phone purchased by him during the Saint-Malo to Portsmouth ferry crossing, and had only been used to contact Wozniak, and to check on train times to London.

Claire continued with her briefing explaining that, as two young Russian soldiers, they had seen active service in Afghanistan, and later in bloody civil conflicts in the Chechen Wars and in Crimea. The latest intelligence identified that both men held the military rank of colonel. Their true birth identity was still in doubt, which was often the case with members in elite Special Forces units. For this reason, and for the purpose of the MI5 investigation, the man would continue to be referred to as Aleksander Kozlowski.

When Wozniak stayed in Peterborough, and the surveillance team member covertly entered his room she found, and left in situ, a loaded German Walther PP pistol hidden in his camera bag, along with a small can of pepper spray, disguised and labelled as a lens cleaner.

The Walther PP is a small personal protection firearm. In contrast, Kozlowski carried a more powerful 9mm semi-automatic GSh-18 gun with armour piercing bullets. The assumption can be made that, in the partnership, Wozniak was responsible for planning and logistics and Kozlowski undertook the actual killing.

The meeting then reviewed the intelligence gathered on the Russian oligarch subject of the assassination plot:

He grew up living in a tenement block on the outskirts of Moscow. His formal education was limited. However, he was considered bright and streetwise. In the chaos of the post-Soviet era, he joined local gangs, becoming a promising entrepreneur involved in black-market activities. He was shrewd and ruthless. Rivals would often disappear, possibly murdered.

He quickly gained vast wealth, and power. He also gained powerful enemies within the criminal and political organisations. It was then time for him to leave Russia. He transferred his money to secret Swiss bank accounts and took up residence in the UK. His wealth was estimated to be over eight billion pounds.

His gated and guarded Chelsea mansion is his home and the operational centre of his international business empire. He remains a very private and secretive person. How he actually acquired his fortune is not known. His transport is an armoured version of the BMW X7 series motor car, built to offer protection against explosives, firearms and attempted kidnapping. Whenever he leaves the security of his home, it is in his chauffeur driven BMW accompanied by two armed body-guards. Additional firepower comes in the form of two Israeli UZI submachine guns, capable of firing two hundred rounds per minute, hidden within the car.

His planned visit to the horse racing stables in Norfolk was arranged some weeks earlier. The time and date were known only to a select few. How the details were leaked was unclear. The suggestion was that communications (telephone and email traffic) emanating from his mansion were routinely monitored. This could easily be achieved by technical resources deployed in the UK, Russia or elsewhere in the world. Previous experience had shown that once a decision is made to eliminate a dissident, the electronic and human resources deployed to achieve it can be large and with a long timescale.

Claire concluded by explaining that research into the men's background and the possibility of their involvement in other assassinations, was ongoing. The distinction, and connection, between Russian government authorised activities and criminal organisation was difficult to ascertain. Often the two elements merged with joint cooperation. The recent spate of assassinations, at the very least, had tacit backing from government officials. Aleksander Kozlowski's paymasters had yet to be confirmed.

When Lawson, during the ferry crossing in his guise as Paul Fisher, had spoken with Kozlowski the man said he had visited the UK several times during his time as a student. Research had failed to identify any previous visits he may have made.

Later during that morning Lawson and Holloway departed from nearby London Heliport on board an Augusta AW 169 twin-engine helicopter. Their destination being a flight across Southern England, and along the coast into the county of Hampshire, landing on the helipad on Saint George's Fort.

The fort is one of four Victorian sea forts built in the Solent between 1865 and 1880 to provide a defence for Portsmouth Harbour against French invasion. The Solent is a major shipping lane for passenger, freight and military vessels. It is also an important recreational area for leisure craft, particularly for yachting. Saint George's Fort is located out at sea about one and a half miles from the Hampshire coast.

The four man-made islands are massive concrete structures over two hundred feet across, with an outer skin of granite blocks. The lower foundation walls are sixty feet thick, rising sixty feet from the sea, clad with heavy iron armour plates all round. In their day, each fort housed a detachment of eighty soldiers and were armed with nine, thirty-ton guns facing seaward and smaller seven-ton guns to the landward side.

The forts are now privately owned luxury homes and hospitality centres. Saint George's is different. It maintains a low profile, purporting to be the private retreat of a wealthy businessman. It is actually owned, maintained and used by the UK intelligence services, including MI5, MI6, Special Forces and senior military personnel.

On landing, Lawson and Holloway were escorted down a flight of stairs to the enclosed main reception area. They anticipated being in residence for several days. The accommodation is luxurious, the equivalent to a top-class hotel.

They were aware that the detainee, Aleksander Kozlowski, had been flown to the fort, from Belmarsh

Prison, two days earlier. He was now accommodated in one of the luxury suites, which consist of a separate lounge and bedroom as well as an en-suite bathroom.

The accommodation was well equipped with expensive toiletries and an extensive library of books, DVD films and music CDs. No newspapers were available and no access to television channels. In effect, it was a luxury cell. All windows were barred and the only door into the suite remained locked.

All activity in the suite was monitored using concealed CCTV cameras relaying live transmission back to the permanently manned Control Centre. He had no access to the outside world. His meals were delivered at set times each day. Staff were under instructions not to communicate with him. Since he had left Belmarsh Prison no personnel had spoken to him, nor indicated why he was there or for how long.

After unpacking and sorting out their own accommodation which, from a previous visit Lawson was aware was less luxurious than the suite occupied by Kozlowski, they visited the Control Centre. There they met with the team undertaking the monitoring. This included a medical doctor, a behavioural expert and an expert in Russian culture and military. Plus, Felix Eastbrook, an MI5 director who they had not previously met.

On the monitors, Kozlowski was observed relaxing and reading a book. He did not appear in the slightest concerned regarding his detention. The doctor reported his heart rate was normal, showing no signs of stress.

The team recommended that he should be left in isolation for a further two days. It was agreed Lawson and Holloway would meet with the team the following morning to discuss interview strategy.

Some months earlier Lawson had spent several days on Saint George's Fort involved in the interrogation of a Russian using the cover name, Lara Zamoyski. She had illegally entered Britain falsely purporting to be Polish and had spent several years assisting ex-KGB members to establish false identities and, thus, able to successfully undertake assassinations.

Eventually, during interrogation, Lara had admitted her involvement in the illegal activities and supplied much useful background information about the operation. However, the following day, whilst still in the luxury accommodation suite she committed suicide by hanging, using a cord from her bathrobe attached to the shower curtain rail.

Being back at the fort, and viewing the suite, reminded Lawson of the sad event. Although he had promised her that cooperation would ensure a comfortable and safe future, Lara believed she would be regarded as a traitor and tracked down and killed. She obviously decided suicide was her only practical option.

Next morning Lawson and Holloway had an early breakfast on the upper terrace of Saint George's Fort before joining the team to review their strategy. It was reported that Kozlowski had slept well and was not showing any signs of concern or stress. It was formally agreed the planned interrogation would commence early the next day.

Lawson and Holloway then visited the Control Centre and met with Director Felix Eastbrook and the other members of the team. They were informed that Director Jane Rigby wished to speak with them via a video conference call. She had with her Claire, a senior intelligence analyst who gave an update on the latest information:

Working with other NATO intelligence agencies British Intelligence had now positively identified the man currently known as Aleksander Kozlowski and his 'London' associate as having been involved, in the recent past, in the suspected deaths of four Russian nationals. In brief:

- Austria. Billionaire oligarch. Apparent heart attack whilst out jogging. Subsequent toxicology report identified he died as the result of poison. The poison has been traced to a Russian military laboratory.
- Berlin. Shooting at close range of a dissident journalist who had sought asylum in Germany. Clearly an execution to send a warning message to others.
- Stockholm. Apparent suicide by hanging of a defector from the Russian military. Toxicology results established he had been sedated prior to death. Forensic examinations showed the method of death could not have been achieved without other human assistance.
- Italy. Billionaire oligarch with known criminal connections. Died in an apparent high speed car crash resulting in the car being destroyed by fire. Subsequent investigations established the man had been sedated prior to death. The car had been deliberately crashed and set on fire.

This was a new and potentially explosive revelation. Up until this time, the only evidence against Kozlowski was his activities in the UK: illegal entry into the UK with a firearm and prohibited ammunition and an intention to commit an assassination.

Now, in each of the four cases mentioned, the relevant authorities had identified that the same two men had entered their respective countries approximately two weeks before each death and left directly afterwards, often departing before the deaths had been reported to the police. Identification of the two was achieved via computer airport passport records and facial recognition analysis, plus, from DNA and fingerprint impressions obtained from forensic examination at the hotels where the men had stayed.

This new information identified their presence in the four countries, but the current evidence so far forthcoming was not confirming they had carried out the killings, although this was the accepted inference. How would this affect the agreed plan for the interrogation of Kozlowski?

On the four assignments, the men had used different identities, with forged Polish passports. Detailed analysis had traced their antecedence back to them being members of the Spetsnaz: Special Operations Forces. This is regarded as Russia's most elite military unit. It is controlled by the main military Intelligence Service.

The conference reviewed the known activities of the two men in the UK and compared them with their visits to the four countries previously mentioned. Some interesting facts emerged. In each case, Jakub Wozniak arrived in the relevant country about two weeks prior to the planned assassination. However, Aleksander Kozlowski would usually arrive only a couple of days before. It was always Wozniak who undertook the necessary monitoring of the target and recognisance of the area.

When Kozlowski had been flown to the fort some three days earlier, the intelligence report identifying his presence in the four countries where killings had occurred, had not been available. At that time, the decision on the interrogation strategy had been based solely on his known actions since arriving in the UK. However, the message from MI5 HQ was that the interrogation should continue.

The character of Kozlowski was discussed. The group agreed he was a man with a strong and determined character. Only the absolute best soldiers are selected to join the Spetsnaz. The military training is long, punishing and brutal, with only a small percentage of recruits being successful. His character, and resolve, would have been further hardened by the years of violent active service in Afghanistan, Chechnya and Crimea.

Director Felix Eastbrook detailed part of the training such soldiers endured. They were taught how to resist interrogation and underwent much brutality to test their psychological and physical ability to withstand not disclosing their identity and useful information to the enemy.

One element of the process involved locking a naked recruit into a small cell for seven days without food. The cell was kept in total darkness and cold. Each day a spray of icy cold water from the ceiling descended down on the shivering and naked recruit. He would quickly learn this was his only means of daily water to drink. If he wished to end the nightmare there was a button to push on the cell door. Activation ended his chances of becoming a prized member of this elite unit.

Felix commented:

"This, perhaps, illustrates why Kozlowski will not be intimidated into confessing by anything the UK Security Service can do to him. We do not employ torture as an interrogation technique. Some of our 'friends' would like to get their hands on him, but I do not believe even 'waterboarding' would persuade him to cooperate."

The behavioural expert added:

"From our experience with recent defectors we have learned that some of the old certainties and loyalties have lessened their commitment to the state. Some of the billionaire oligarchs have military or political backgrounds: greed now being their main goal. Others, like Kozlowski, may regard them as traitors to the state and hunt them. Similarly, they may sell their services to a dubious criminal organisation and still hunt them. Greed, resentment and jealousy have entered the equation."

The expert explained the rationale behind placing Kozlowski in luxury, but secure and isolated, accommodation:

"For several days he is receiving five-star hotel treatment. He has failed in his mission to complete an assassination. His masters will not be pleased. Currently, they do not know what has happened to him. One thing for sure; they will disown him and will never publicly admit that he is, or was, one of their own."

Mark Holloway asked: "Does he have a choice?"

Felix Eastbrook responded:

"His options are limited. We have the evidence, and as a last resort, he can be convicted of the crime and spend the rest of his life in a UK prison, or we hand him over to one of the other countries where he has allegedly committed murder. I would suggest his best option would be to fully cooperate with us, no holds barred, and we would consider immunity and place him on the rehabilitation programme. A new identity, plastic surgery, relocation to a friendly country and a reasonable pension from HM Government for life. Take your pick Mr Aleksander Kozlowski."

Lawson, with a cynical grin, added:

"And my job is to tell him to be a good boy and cooperate. Sounds easy."

The team agreed that although a formal interrogation room was available within the fort, the appropriate approach should begin with a more relaxed interview taking place in the lounge of his accommodation. Initially Lawson would go in alone. Kozlowski still did not know that the man he had befriended as Paul Fisher was actually Lawson.

When Kozlowski was incarcerated in Belmarsh Prison he had shared his meal and exercise breaks with a fellow detainee who, he thought, was in a similar position to himself. The man was actually an MI5 operative, who reported back that Kozlowski had expressed regret that the innocent man he had befriended on the ferry had been arrested with him and subjected to a beating by the police. Hopefully, this was a good sign for the forthcoming interview.

The behavioural expert gave his final assessment and advice:

"This man will not be intimidated. He will not respond well to threats. Do not demean him by your words or manner. He is your prisoner, and he will resent that. He is proud of his ability and requires from a fellow intelligence officer respect for his professionalism, albeit he will regard you as his enemy. He will carefully judge you. He will consider he is your equal. Before you speak, he will know what you are attempting to achieve. He knows his value. Let him know you value him. At the end of the process, he will consciously decide whether it is worth negotiating his future. Good luck for tomorrow."

Lawson made a last comment:

"Now we suspect that Kozlowski has also possibly committed murder in four countries, I don't feel morally, or legally, comfortable introducing the suggestion that he may be eligible for the 'rehabilitation programme.' I won't mention that during the initial meeting with him".

The next day dawned. Lawson and Holloway together had a 07:00 hours cooked breakfast and discussed the plan for the day. Initially Lawson would interview Kozlowski alone with Holloway monitoring the progress in the Control Centre and be prepared to undertake research if required.

At 08:00 hours both entered the Control Centre and spent ten minutes observing Kozlowski via the monitors. He was up and dressed and had finished his light Continental breakfast. It was time to begin the interview.

The door to the accommodation suite was unlocked. Lawson slowly and deliberately walked in and sat down. He said nothing and just looked at Kozlowski for a minute or more. Kozlowski was seated on the settee. He remained motionless, just looking straight into the eyes of Lawson.

"Good morning Aleksander." Lawson was now clean shaven with short hair, wearing a dark navy city style suit; different in appearance to when he last saw Kozlowski using the identity, Paul Fisher.

"Who are you?" came the response in an angry voice.

"I am an MI5 officer."

"Your name?"

"That is not relevant."

"Your rank?"

"Likewise, that is not relevant for the present."

Both remained seated, motionless and looking directly at each other.

Lawson broke the awkwardness with a mild smile:

"I know your true name is not Aleksander Kozlowski. We have identified you visiting different countries using various false aliases. So, to keep things simple, for the present I will continue to address you as Aleksander."

Kozlowski made no reply. He clearly recognised Lawson as the man he had befriended on the ferry.

Lawson continued:

"We may be on different sides, Aleksander, but I am hoping we do not have to be enemies. My people have been extremely busy, in recent weeks, research-ing your background. You have an impressive history. We know all about you, from your recruitment to the Spetsnaz Special Operations Forces, to your war record in Afghanistan, to the wars in Chechnya and Crimea. I even have a newspaper photograph of you in Crimea being presented with a hero's medal by President Putin."

Lawson took a copy of the photograph from his case and placed it on the coffee table.

Kozlowski remained motionless. Not a glimmer of a response.

Lawson did not speak for a minute or more, then continued:

"We have been liaising with our intelligence col-leagues in various NATO countries and have identified where you and your friend, Jakub Wozniak, have vis-ited together."

Still no response. Lawson had been prepared for this to be a long process. He would be patient and re-membered the advice the behavioural scientist had given him.

Lawson sat and remained silent. He sensed Kozlow-ski's eyes moving and clearly assessing the situation he found himself in.

Kozlowski was also assessing Lawson. He was wear-ing a well-cut suit with expensive black leather brogue shoes and wearing on his left wrist a luxury watch. On his lap was resting a brown leather-bound notebook and he was holding a black and gold Montblanc ball-point pen. This suggested to Kozlowski that Lawson was an MI5 officer of senior rank. There was a satisfaction that Kozlowski's position demanded he be dealt with by a man of senior rank.

Lawson leaned forward and in a quiet voice said:

"Your friend Jakub is back in Belarus. He is actually staying in the Security Service HQ in Minsk. Your bosses do not know where you are."

Still no response from Kozlowski, although Lawson sensed he was becoming more relaxed.

Lawson considered it time to inject a surprise into proceedings and see Kozlowski's reaction.

"When you two visited four countries within Europe the suspicious deaths of four Russian nationals occurred. Four deaths, or more correctly, four assassinations."

Lawson took from his brief case a printed schedule and placed it on the coffee table in front of Kozlowski. It was an analysis chart comparing information received from the four countries regarding the visits undertaken by Kozlowski and Wozniak. Lawson sat back in his chair and remained silent. Kozlowski showed no emotion or interest in the schedule. Both men sat motionless for a good ten minutes. Who was going to make the first move?

Finally, Lawson stood up: "Let's take a break."

He walked over to the locked door. He knocked and it was opened by a guard. Lawson left. The door was closed and locked. Lawson went into the Control Centre and joined Holloway who was viewing the monitors. Kozlowski remained seated but was now looking intently at the schedule. He did not handle it.

Lawson and Holloway adjourned for an early lunch on the upper terrace with its unobscured view out to sea. They discussed the morning's events and were considering the afternoon's approach to the interview with Kozlowski, when a member of staff interrupted with an urgent message: Director Felix Eastbrook was being recalled to MI5 HQ. No further interview with Kozlowski must take place. They were to abort current plans and wait until Eastbrook returned.

Lawson looked at Holloway and shrugged his shoulders:

"I wonder what that's about. We wait for Felix's return with interest."

With no immediate work, they decided to relax and stay a little longer on the terrace enjoying the sea view and drinking another glass of wine.

Late evening, they receive a message: Eastbrook had spent the afternoon in conference with senior government ministers. The helicopter was not equipped for flying at night, nor were night landings on the fort's helipad permitted, so he would not be back until the morning.

Eastbrook arrived back on the fort and called an 08:00 hours meeting in the conference room. Lawson, Holloway and the other members of the team attended. Eastbrook was in his normal polite and friendly mood, but it was evident that he was feeling exasperated by the events of the previous afternoon. Coffee was served.

He took a large unopened bottle of single malt whisky from his briefcase:

"I don't normally advocate alcohol when working, but there are times in life when the rules need to be broken. Please help yourself to a whisky with your coffee. I'm going to have one."

Each of the team take turns to take the bottle and enhance their coffee with a whisky.

"To break another rule, I am going to be critical of our political masters. It appears the proverbial has hit the fan, and some of it has stuck."

Eastbrook shook his head, took a sip of his coffee, and continued:

"I spent the afternoon with a senior cabinet minister. New in her role. Only recently obtained her Enhanced Security grade, which allows me to even discuss these matters with her. She has no previous working knowledge or experience on national security matters, yet I had to listen to her diatribe on the rights and wrongs of British Intelligence."

He took a pause and continued:

"Political interference usually means confusion and trouble. Decisions are based on self-interest and the need for media attention. The minister now strongly objects to the previously agreed approach for dealing with Kozlowski. She refuses to take into account the view of the Service, based on our collective professional knowledge and expertise."

Eastbrook reported, in detail, on his discussion with the minister. She instructed that Kozlowski must be returned to Belmarsh Prison without delay with the case being formally signed over to the police. He would be initially charged with illegal entry to the UK using a forged passport and with unlawful possession of a 'section one' firearm and prohibited ammunition. He would be remanded in custody, back to Belmarsh Prison, with the court informed that police investigations were continuing with the likelihood of further charges being brought relating to an attempt to assassinate a Russian oligarch resident in the UK.

Eastbrook accepted that the new intelligence, regarding Kozlowski's suspected involvement in the four successful assassinations, meant the case should rightly be handed over to the police to deal with the crimes committed in the UK. No doubt, dealing with extradition requests from the four identified countries would take up much legal time and expense.

His objection was the minister's insistence that she would speak with the Press to disclose details about 'the arrest of a suspected assassin entering the UK to murder a Russian oligarch' and linking it with assassinations of other Russian nationals in other European countries. He considered this unprofessional, unnecessary and potentially damaging to ongoing investigations by the Security Service. He suggested it was purely reflecting her own self-importance with such media coverage.

Eastbrook explained that he had spoken with the senior police officer who would be taking charge of the case. MI5 would continue to have access to Kozlowski in an effort to develop intelligence. Such meetings, with any intelligence obtained, would not form any element of the police case against Kozlowski and certainly would not be presented in a court of law.

Kozlowski remained a potentially important source of intelligence for MI5. No doubt, in the future, there would be further attempts to assassinate Russian nationals' resident in the UK and abroad. British Intelligence had a duty to identify the centre of the operation which, without much doubt, was controlled from Moscow and to identify the 'Sponsors'.

The helicopter to take Kozlowski back to Belmarsh Prison would not be arriving until the afternoon. Permission was granted for Lawson and Holloway to conduct a final interview to gauge what cooperation he might be willing to give. No mention of the rehabilitation programme or promises would be on the agenda.

At 11:00 hours Lawson and Holloway visited Kozlowski in his accommodation suite. He appeared subdued and not in a mood to communicate.

On entering the room Lawson spoke:

"Good morning Colonel. I trust you had a good night's sleep. Won't be spending much time with you today."

He had deliberately addressed him as 'Colonel' to let Kozlowski know they now had a detailed knowledge of his background but, more importantly, to indicate a degree of respect. Kozlowski was a proud man and respect was important to his ego.

Lawson was open in explaining what was going to happen, with Kozlowski being handed over to the police. He further added their contact would, hopefully, continue with Lawson making occasional visits to Belmarsh Prison.

Lawson continued:

"The role of MI5 is the gathering of intelligence to protect the integrity and safety of the United Kingdom. We do not have the authority to prosecute people. That is the role of the police. Details of this, and any future conversations we may have, will not be presented as evidence in any British court of law. Aleksander, is there any benefit in us continuing this conversation now and conversations in the future?"

Again, this approach was a deliberate policy to make Kozlowski feel he was an equal and important part of the conversation.

Kozlowski nodded in apparent agreement. After a pause he spoke:

"You regard me as an assassin, a violent killer. No. I am a disciplined and professional soldier. I am proud to serve my country and eliminate our enemies. Your SAS go to Iran, fight in a war and kill your enemies and are called heroes. What is the difference?"

Holloway asked:

"Are you acknowledging you came to the UK on an assassination mission and were also involved in the four deaths outlined in the schedule?"

Kozlowski responded:

"I have no need to play these games with you. I neither admit nor deny my involvement. It is sufficient to say I am proud of the service I have given my country. Why do you spend so much effort protecting these villains and traitors? How does a man suddenly become a multi-billionaire? He does it by corruption and stealing vast public assets of the State, then hiding away the billions of dollars in secret Swiss bank accounts. Then runs away to your country to live a life of super luxury. They are traitors who deserve to be tracked down and eliminated: and their vast wealth returned to the Russian people."

Kozlowski clearly considered that he had been serving his country honourably. He was an intelligent man, who clearly knew how the game of espionage is played out. He indicated, in further verbal exchanges, that he was willing to bide his time in prison as he 'might prove useful' for a future prisoner exchange. This was a proven strategy.

At some stage in the future, it was likely an innocent businessman or tourist would be detained on a trumped-up charge of espionage. Then via back-channel messages, insisting no publicity is given in the media, indicate a swap would be possible in exchange for one of their imprisoned agents. He did not feel he would remain in a British or European prison for too long. He was probably correct. Kozlowski certainly wasn't prepared to 'roll over' and betray his motherland to the perceived enemy.

Lawson and Holloway prepared to conclude the meeting. Lawson shook him by the hand and said:

"Goodbye. I wish you well my friend." Again, a deliberate act intended to sow the seeds of goodwill for future meetings between the two.

Next day Lawson and Holloway were back at MI5 HQ attending a meeting with Director Jane Rigby, where a briefing on the outcome of Operation Backfire was discussed. It would remain an active investigation being undertaken by the police. At an appropriate time, Lawson would seek an update from the police and then consider whether to visit Kozlowski in Belmarsh Prison.

CHAPTER FIVE

Operation Blowtorch

Lawson was woken by the sound of his iPhone ringing. He glanced at the clock on his bedside table. It was only 02:20 hours. He took a moment to gather his thoughts, then turned on the sidelight, sat up in bed and feeling slightly grumpy answered the phone. It was Mark Holloway calling. Mark explained that he had been designated to call the team together for a 'breaking incident.' At this time, he had few details, other than it was terrorist related. The team was being requested to meet up at a private country house hotel in Wiltshire. The address was given, and Lawson was asked to be there as soon as practicable. No further reason was given.

Lawson arrived at the country house hotel and parked his Land Rover Defender truck. The hotel is located in its own extensive grounds. It was immediately apparent, the hotel was subject to security arrangements, not normally expected for this type of establishment. There was a military vehicle parked outside. Two armed soldiers were standing at the entrance, with a list of names, and were checking identification before allowing people into the hotel.

On entering the reception area, he was directed to the ground-floor conference room. He quickly learned that the hotel was closed to normal guests, due to renovation work, and had been hired, at extremely short notice, for the exclusive use of MI5. He had yet to be told the reason. He met up with Mark Holloway and four other members of the team. All were as puzzled as Lawson as to why they have been called together, at this unearthly hour, at an hotel miles from anywhere. In times of a major incident, it is not unusual for a law enforcement or government agency to deploy, at short notice, to an available establishment such as a hotel or conference centre.

Director Jane Rigby eventually entered the conference room. She acknowledged she had been at the hotel for several hours, working in a first-floor room, with several other technical staff, setting up a 'mini' communications facility. The current information remained limited.

Rigby explained that intelligence had been intercepted to strongly indicate a major terrorist attack is planned for later in the day. The exact location was currently unknown, but the target was likely to be a significant government building within the City. Hence, the reason why MI5 HQ London had been closed to staff. Other departments of the service had been deployed to surrounding army bases and police headquarters. The matter had been given the title, Operation Blowtorch.

A government COBRA meeting was scheduled to be held at 08:00 hours. It was to be chaired by a senior Cabinet minister. COBRA stands for Cabinet Office Briefing Room A. It is the government's Civil Contingencies Committee, which is located in the Cabinet Office in Whitehall. It is convened to handle matters of a national emergency or major disruption and coordinates different departments and agencies to respond to such emergencies. A top official from MI5 will attend the meeting.

The current threat level in the UK was at SEVERE. The judgement for this level was on the basis of available intelligence, that an attack was highly likely. With such matters the police have the lead role. The role of MI5 is in intelligence gathering. The various police and intelligence agencies in the UK work closely together in the fight against terrorism. In recent years, many plots have successfully been disrupted. Most are not reported in the Press.

It had been estimated that over four hundred UK extremists had recently returned home after fighting in Syria and Iraq. The majority would have received combat and terrorist training, and additionally would be motivated by their experiences. They presented a significant threat to the safety and security of the UK. Other British individuals had been radicalised online inspired by the, so called, Islamic State.

Currently, there was no positive identification of two of the suspected six terrorists believed to be involved in today's planned attack. The two British born men are known to have travelled to Syria and actively fought for the, so-called, Islamic State. They returned to the UK posing as refugees, escaping the conflict, aboard a rubber dingy which came ashore along the coast of Southern England. They were among a group of fourteen 'refugees' including women and children. The two men alleged they did not speak English. On being detained they were taken to a holding centre in Kent but quickly disappeared and were not seen again.

Throughout the morning intensive human and technical resources, from the various intelligence agencies, were deployed to actively monitor telephone and Internet communications in an attempt to identify and then trace the location of the terrorists. Director Jane Rigby asked Lawson and Holloway to travel to the temporary Command Headquarters, set up in London, to run the operation. They were to act as liaison between the MI5 and the police.

By midday, it was confirmed that there were three active teams of terrorists, with two terrorists in each team. Each team was travelling in a van. At this time, the make and type of vans being used was not known. The terrorists use of their iPhones was deliberately infrequent, making monitoring and tracking of their locations extremely difficult. The exact location of any of the three teams had not been ascertained. However, they appeared to be converging towards London. Extensive and coordinated research, with active monitoring, was continuing.

The first team, with the van containing the two identified men, was being driven from the direction of

North Wales. The intelligence indicated they had spent the past few days camping in a remote disused quarry, preparing and practicing for the forthcoming attack. There was no intelligence to suggest other members of the group had been with them at the quarry. Communications emanating from them had been, and continued to be, limited. They were using cheap pay-as-you-go iPhones, which significantly reduced the likelihood of identifying the subscriber.

In the build up to this planned attack, the two men's presence on the Dark Web had been identified and monitored. The Dark Web is a hidden collective of Internet sites, only accessible by a specialised web browser, used to keep the internet activity anonymous and private. It has become the chosen forum for terrorist propaganda, and contact for illegal activity and, importantly, for funding terrorism.

Intelligence indicated that two individuals in the second team are also British born and fought in Syria alongside the two men in the first group. The identity of the men in the second group was not known. From previous technical monitoring of their telephone contact with the first group, voice analysis had been obtained.

The two members of the third group were not believed to have fought abroad in a terrorist capacity. Indications were that they were 'home-grown', having been radicalised from use of Internet Islamic State propaganda. The least information was known about this third group.

The first two-man team, in this group of three teams, was considered to be the leading dominant team. They were clearly the team undertaking the planning and giving the orders on the proposed action and deployment.

It was 13:30 hours. Significant progress continued to be made. The van containing the first team was stationary at a service station on the M4 motorway near Newbury. The two suspects were sitting on a bench nearby. One was currently talking on his iPhone. The van was a dark blue coloured Ford Transit. The telephone call was being monitored via technical resources. A surveillance team was now in position at the service station, with covert photographs of the suspects and van having been obtained.

The terrorist's telephone was being used to connect with two other pay-as-you-go mobile phones. The calls were being kept deliberately short to avoid being traced. The terrorists were surveillance aware. The monitoring agency had been able to identify that the signals from the two other mobile phones were emanating from the London area. Voice analysis confirmed, in both cases, the persons receiving the calls were the same men who have been in previous telephone contact with the two men in the first team.

Options were now being considered by the senior strategic team at the temporary Command HQ. Currently, the first team of two terrorists had been fully identified. They were away from their vehicle, sitting away from the public and under surveillance. There was a team of Special Forces personnel nearby who could quickly take the two suspects into custody. However, the identity and exact location of the other two teams was still unknown. Therefore, detaining the first two terrorists would not eliminate the continuing danger from the second and third teams.

The decision was to authorise the operation to continue. When the first terrorist team decided to move from the service station area, they would be covertly followed by the Special Forces group and also be the subject of intense technical surveillance.

The first terrorist team remained at the service station for over sixty minutes. Several short telephone calls were made to each of the two other terrorist teams. The conversations were guarded in their content, with no direct mention of their intention to undertake terrorist attacks.

They casually mentioned 'the party' being at 16:30 hours, and with the second team 'visiting Oxford Street.' The third team mentioned 'looking at number ten.' The three teams also confirmed they would be wearing their 'party dresses.' This was taken as a reference that they would be wearing suicide vests, which they intended to detonate during their attacks.

Earlier intelligence had already indicated MI5 HQ was likely to be a target. Now, the intercepted telephone communications had indicated that targets two and three would be Whitehall and the busy Oxford Street. The top strategic team was working on the assumption that the terrorists are planning to carry out multiple attacks and coordinate all to be undertaken at 16:30 hours today.

More intelligence was forthcoming. The Ford Transit van being used by the first team was hired five days earlier from a car hire company in Birmingham. It had now been established that false details were supplied during the vehicle hire. Rather carelessly, but extremely fortunate for the current investigation, two other Ford Transit vans were also hired within the same time frame. The documents used were also false. Details, including registration numbers, of the two vans had been passed to the operations Command HQ.

It was now approaching 16:00 hours. Active and intensive monitoring of radio and telephone frequencies was continuing. The SAS, other Special Forces personnel and police tactical firearms teams had been briefed and deployed to various locations in the London area.

The three terrorist Ford Transit vans had now been identified, with their current moving locations pinpointed. All three vans were heading towards London. The vehicles were initially picked up by the use of ANPR (Automatic Number Plate Recognition) technology, which operate at fixed locations, alongside CCTV cameras. The system instantly checks against database records for vehicles of interest. The operations Command HQ team was now physically monitoring the movement of all three vehicles.

The first terrorist van was travelling on the M1 motorway east towards London. The second van was travelling south on the M1 motorway towards London. The third van was travelling on the M11 motorway west towards London.

A final briefing and discussion were taking place with the senior strategic team at Command HQ. Positive identification for four of the terrorists had been made. Although the identity of the other two had still not been established, their link with the other four had. The intelligence and physical surveillance had established all six were armed.

The intention of the six was to carry out a marauding terrorist firearms attack in the City. Their aim was to kill. The communications intercepts indicated each was wearing an explosive device in the form of a suicide vest. The location of their three intended targets was also evident from the telephone intercepts.

The decision was made to simultaneously intercept the three Ford Transit vans, before they reached their intended destinations and, thus, neutralise the threat to the public. As is the agreed protocol in such matters, written authority was signed to formally transfer command of the next phase of the operation to the senior commanding army officer present at Command HQ.

The three Transit vans, containing the six terrorists, were now about three miles from their intended targets. Progress was slow in the late afternoon traffic. This was of benefit to the 'hunters.' The order was given for the military Special Forces interception teams to commence their deployment. The method was effective and unobtrusive, not raising any suspicion from the terrorists or other road users.

Behind each of the separately travelling Transit vans, an anonymous grey coloured Range Rover four-by-four, with dark tinted side and rear windows, pulled out from a side road to join the flow of traffic and follow immediately behind. Such vehicles are a common sight in Central London.

A little further on, a second Range Rover discreetly joined the slow-moving traffic behind the first Range Rover. Behind the second Range Rover a nondescript Transit van subsequently slots in behind. With about a mile for each of the three terrorist vehicles to travel, a large furniture type van pulled out of a side road, and in front of each, into the flow of traffic.

The technical support team at Command HQ flicked a switch to temporarily block any outgoing or incoming communication on the terrorists' iPhones. Traffic lights on the three routes were now being controlled from Command HQ. The command team had a clear visual view from the CCTV monitors of the three terrorist vans and the following military vehicles.

The progress of the three convoys, with the sequencing of the traffic lights and the furniture vans setting the pace, was firmly under the control of Command HQ and the senior military Commander. The military Commander calmly looked around the room. He asked if everything was in place, and everyone was ready. He checked that the operational teams were ready to proceed. All nodded in agreement. He raised his right index finger:

"Good hunting everyone. STRIKE, STRIKE, STRIKE."

At each location, the leading furniture van was now stationary at the controlled set of traffic lights. As the lights changed to green, in a coordinated set of movements, the first Range Rover quickly accelerated forward to the right and closed along-side the terrorist's Transit van. The second Range Rover veered forward and to the left and stops alongside the Transit van. At the same moment, the furniture van backed deliberately into the front of the terrorist's van, with the following military Transit van slamming heavily into the back of the terrorist's van, which is now boxed in on all four sides.

This front and back shunt manoeuvre disorientated the two terrorists inside the van. Instantly, a powerful stun grenade smashed the driver's side window and exploded in the cab with a deafening thud, followed by a short burst of rapid gunfire. The terrorists did not have the opportunity to use their weapons, nor detonate their suicide vests.

The military operation was completed with surgical precision. No doubt, it had been rehearsed over and over again on some deserted military airfield.

It was all over in a matter of seconds. A shattering of noise and energy, followed by silence. The same scenario, with the same result, had taken place at the three locations: Whitehall, Victoria Embankment and Oxford Street.

The intention of the terrorists had been to cause mass carnage and fear. The swift and professional response by the various agencies stopped that taking place. No member of the public had been injured.

A simple message from each of the three military teams was radioed back to their Commander at Command HQ:

"Terrorist first team. Neutralised."

"Terrorist second team. Neutralised."

"Terrorist third team. Neutralised."

The Commanding officer, in an extremely professional and understated manner simply replies:

"Splendid work. I'll see you back at the holding base."

He handed the written authority back to the senior police officer present in the Command Centre, smiled and said:

"It's been a pleasure to do business with you." He then left the building.

At each of the three locations, the respective military teams quickly departed and returned to their holding base at nearby Regent's Park Barracks. A team of police officers would be present to take written witness statements from the military personnel involved in the three operations. The statements would be required at the Coroner's Inquest into the deaths of the six terrorists. Identities of the soldiers involved in the killings would not be disclosed.

Backup support teams of police personnel moved into the three locations. The necessary forensic photographs are taken. A doctor, attached to each of the three support teams, confirms the terrorists are dead.

The three damaged terrorist Transit vans were then covered with large tarpaulin sheets and hoisted onto recovery trucks. The bodies of the dead terrorists remained in the Transit vans as they were taken back to secure premises for forensic examination.

The police Counter-Terrorism Department's investigation into this terrorist cell would continue for several months. There would be close working liaison between the department and MI5. Lawson and Holloway would remain at the temporary Command HQ for several days working with the team.

Chapter Six

Blackmail and Spying

Director Jane Rigby said she had a new case involving espionage for Julian Lawson and Mark Holloway to investigate. Julian would be the lead case officer.

With all matters reviewed and undertaken by MI5 no one individual would know the complete circumstances of a case. The policy is that staff dealing with a case only know the intelligence that is required to successfully complete the element for which they are commissioned to investigate. This method protects the integrity of an investigation, so if one part is compromised the other elements remain secure and the damage is limited.

What is espionage? In recent years, the public's perception of MI5 is of an organisation that is mainly involved in the pursuit of terrorists. MI5 is the United Kingdom's domestic counter-intelligence and security agency. The service is directed to protect British democracy and economic interests, and counter terrorism and espionage within the United Kingdom.

Espionage or spying is: 'the act of obtaining secret or confidential information or divulging of the same without permission of the holder of the information.' Counter-espionage remains an important function within MI5.

An individual or spy ring can commit espionage. The practice is clandestine. Espionage is a method of gathering information from various sources. One of the most effective ways to gather data and information about a targeted organisation is by infiltrating its ranks. This is the job of the spy. Information collection techniques used in the conduct of clandestine human intelligence include operational techniques, asset recruiting and tradecraft.

Director Jane Rigby gave an overview of the case to Lawson and Holloway: The identity of the source, as was normal service procedure, would remain only known to his MI5 handlers. He was a defector, having been recruited by British Intelligence, and given the pseudonym Springwatch.

Springwatch had been a major in the Russian Federal Counterintelligence Service (FSK), formerly known as the KGB. His last posting had been a three-year secondment at the Russian embassy of a Scandinavian country.

It had been a long, complicated and sensitive recruitment process. Some two years earlier British Intelligence identified that he appeared disgruntled with his employers. He displayed several character weaknesses, including enjoying the new freedom and luxury he found in the Scandinavian way of life.

He had previously served at the Russian Embassy in London as the number three in the hierarchy of the FSK team, so would have a good knowledge of covert operations carried out against the interests of the United Kingdom.

Early in the delicate recruitment process, it was known that he was extremely unhappy that he had not received further promotion and was nearing retirement. He did not enjoy the prospect of returning to Moscow to spend his retirement in his small government owned apartment. He was the ideal candidate for recruitment, and so it proved.

Intricate plans were put in place, with British Intelligence, to facilitate his disappearance from the embassy without undue suspicion. At the beginning of a scheduled week's leave, he announced it was his intention to spend several days walking, and camping overnight, on the local mountain range.

As soon as he was safely away from the embassy he was spirited out of the country. High up in the mountains his equipment was left in such a manner that it would be found after a search, but to suggest he had met with an accident and disappeared down one of the deep gullies. The matter was reported in the local press, simply that a member of embassy staff had gone missing in the mountains and presumed to have met with an accident. No evidence had been put forward to suggest he had defected.

He had now spent six months housed at a secret and secure location, in the north of England, undergoing extensive debriefing by British Intelligence. At the outset, he had been guaranteed immunity from prosecution and offered protection under the 'rehabilitation programme.'

An extensive file had been compiled on the intelligence he had supplied. It detailed covert activities, undertaken over many years in the UK. British nationals had been successfully recruited to betray classified and secret information surreptitiously obtained from their respective employment. This included gleaning information from sources connected to the military, economic, political and social sectors.

Lawson and Holloway would initially deal with one element of the intelligence, regarding military secrets obtained on the sea trials of a new class of British built submarine. The file detailed how the subject had been recruited, what information he was required to illicitly obtain, how it was transferred to his Russian Intelligence handler and what his reward was. The operation remained active, with the subject still supplying information. He was not aware his activities had been uncovered by British Intelligence. Lawson and Holloway would undertake investigations into the British subject and, eventually, undertake his interrogation.

The nuclear-powered submarines were being constructed at a major shipbuilding British facility. The first of the new class of submarines was launched in the early years of the twenty-first century. The submarines are the largest and most advanced attack submarines ever built for the British Royal Navy. They form a vital part of the defence of the UK. Their weapons include a mix of heavy Spearfish torpedoes and Tomahawk cruise missiles. The submarines are designed to circumnavigate the globe submerged, producing their own oxygen and drinking water. The Russian intelligence mission, which had been active for several years, was to obtain detailed secret data on the sea-trials.

The identified subject is a Steven William Archer, forty-two years of age and a married man. He is a senior IT manager employed with a company that undertakes work for defence contractors. Archer had been illicitly supplying secret information to Russian Intelligence for many years. How was he recruited and why was he willing to embark on this traitorous and dangerous activity?

The recruitment process began slowly, and innocently, without him realising what was happening. A classic 'KGB' style long-term trap.

As a teenage student at Oxford, a tutor with Marxist sympathies, identified Archer as a likely candidate to the Russian cause. A friendship developed with the tutor introducing Archer to his associates and joining in with their social activities. A group holiday was undertaken, visiting a former Soviet country. Much alcohol was consumed at several all-night riotous parties. Archer's recollection of the activities at the parties remains vague.

Several years later, he was a young graduate recruit employed by an established company involved in managing defence contracts. He was by now happily married and life was good. He had continued his platonic friendship with one of the men from his student days. His friend needed a 'favour' for some information from Archer's place of employment. The information was not classified, but it was against the rules. Further occasional requests followed. Slowly, the information requested became more important and small cash payments were his reward.

Then, one evening Archer was invited by his friend to his apartment and introduced to two associates. Whisky was poured; laughter and easy conversation flowed. One of the associates spoke about their fun holidays as students. Photographs of their holidays were produced and handed around. Colour photographs, in excellent clarity, of the group hill walking. Then photographs taken at their all-night parties. The definition was equally good.

The laughter suddenly stopped. Archer was holding in his hands and staring in disbelief at the content. It was of three naked men having full sex together. He was one of the men. Without words being said, further photographs were passed to him. Each more graphic and disgusting. The trap had closed. Co-operate or face humiliation and disgrace.

That meeting had occurred fifteen years ago. The memory remained very fresh in his mind. He had co-operated since that date. The information demanded from his 'controllers' became ever more serious. Archer continued climbing the ladder of promotion. In his senior position he was now supplying classified and secret information. For several years he had supplied sensitive information on the sea-trials of the new nuclear powered British submarine.

He was now being paid significant amounts of cash for his services. His senior position, with the appropriate security clearance level, gave him the necessary unsupervised access to the relevant computer systems. He would download the secret reports onto a computer stick. The method of getting the information to his handler was 'old fashioned' but effective. Early each Sunday morning he would leave his home in Brockenhurst, in the county of Hampshire, to take his Cocker Spaniel dog, Daisy, for a walk through the nearby New Forest. It was always at the same time on the same day.

On reaching a certain point along the woodland track, he would turn left and walk twenty yards through the bracken to a rotting log, which he lifted. Taking the computer stick, which was in a plastic case, from his jacket pocket, he placed it under the log. From the same location he retrieved a plastic wallet containing cash in Bank of England notes. Normally, that was £1000 per visit.

He had never met his Russian handler. Unknown to Archer, the handler would always place the money under the log thirty minutes before he was due to arrive. The handler would then remain out of sight secretly observing the arrival of Archer and then, once he had left, retrieve the computer stick.

If Archer felt there was a need to speak with his handler, and the instruction was that this must only be for an extreme emergency, he would leave a ten-pence coin with the computer stick. The handler would then telephone him on his iPhone whilst Archer was still walking in the woodland. Archer did not possess the contact details of his handler. When the handler telephoned Archer the telephone number did not appear on his screen, it had been deliberately blocked.

When British Intelligence identified what Archer was doing, immediate steps were taken to stop further damage being caused. The technical department took control to monitor all his computer activities and ensure all future downloads of sea-trials contained incorrect information. His weekly Sunday morning trips to the New Forest were allowed to continue under covert surveillance. This action enabled the Surveillance Team to video the visits and identify the Russian handler.

Early Monday morning, Archer was walking from Victoria Railway Station, across St James's Park, when he was intercepted by Lawson and Holloway. Brief introductions were made, and he was asked to join them to sit on a nearby park bench. Lawson repeated that they were MI5 officers and needed to speak with him, in some detail, at their London office. Archer responded that he was too busy and suggested they contact his secretary to make an appointment with him at a later convenient date.

Lawson responded: "You do not appear to realise the seriousness of the situation. We need to speak with you now."

"What's this about?"

"I'm not prepared to go into detail sitting in the centre of St James's Park. I will once again ask you to come with us."

Archer asked: "If I decline will you arrest me?"

"No. Members of MI5 do not possess the power to arrest. That remains the prerogative of the police."

"In that case I will decline your request. Please contact my secretary to arrange an appointment." Archer got up and was about to walk away.

Lawson gently placed a hand on Archer's shoulder:

"There is an alternative, but it is an unpleasant and embarrassing one. At the crack of dawn several police cars, plus a prison van, all with blue lights flashing, will arrive outside your home address waking up your neighbours. You will be arrested, handcuffed and marched out to the prison van, all being watched by your neighbours and upsetting your family. I recommend you come quietly with us now."

He reluctantly agreed. The three walked to their car which was parked nearby. Lawson drove, with Holloway sitting in the rear with Archer.

As they drove slowly along The Mall with Buckingham Palace in view, Holloway commented:

"The Royal Standard is flying. Her Majesty is in residence. Makes me proud to be British and to know our country is being defended by our brave soldiers, airmen and sailors." His words were said with a large hint of sarcasm and irony.

The car parked at the rear of Admiralty House in Horse Guards Parade. The front of the building faces Whitehall. Discreetly located on the second floor of the building, with no outward sign of its function, is the interviewing suite of MI5. Entry is gained via a heavy oak door which was unlocked and opened by a suited middle-aged man: no doubt, ex-military. Lawson showed his identity. Their arrival had been expected.

The three visitors were escorted to the Lord Nelson Room. Each of several rooms within the complex is named after a historic Naval admiral. The room was furnished with solid Victorian leather-bound chairs and a large impressive looking desk. Lawson could imagine it previously being the desk of a heroic admiral. He made himself comfortable behind the desk and gestured to Archer to take a seat in front of him. Holloway sat alongside Lawson.

Archer looked ill at ease. A member of staff entered and served coffee. Lawson was aware that the interview would be covertly recorded. He had undertaken several previous interviews in this room. Some members referred to them as interrogations. He preferred the word 'interview'. He was in no rush to begin. Silence is often the most powerful incentive to elicit the truth. He sipped his coffee and looked at Archer. He did not smile nor offer any facial sign of reassurance.

Finally, Lawson spoke: "Mr Archer, why do you think you are here?"

"I haven't a clue."

"We're members of the Security Service, MI5. The domestic intelligence service for the United Kingdom. One of our roles is to protect the State against external threats from foreign enemies. The term countering Espionage figures large in our armoury. We are here to discuss a serious matter."

Lawson took a pause and appeared to change the subject:

"What did you do yesterday? Sunday was a lovely sunny day."

"In the morning I took my dog for a walk in the New Forest. Home for lunch with my family, then a relaxing afternoon in the garden."

Lawson continued:

"Please be aware, we do not deal in rumour or speculation. We only deal with facts. We never interview anyone until we have the facts and the evidence."

He left a space for a long silence. Then leaned forward, towards Archer, resting both arms on the desk:

"Did anything important happen yesterday?"

"No."

Lawson, still leaning forward spoke deliberately and quietly:

"What about the one thousand pounds your handler left under the log for you?"

Archer did not reply. His right foot had begun to shake. He was now looking nervous.

Lawson spoke: "I make no apology if you feel uncomfortable. How would you describe yourself?"

"I'm sorry." Archer was endeavouring not to make eye contact with his interrogator.

"The law would describe you as a traitor. For many years you have been betraying your country, selling national secrets for financial gain. Why?"

"They blackmailed me. They promised to ruin me unless I did what they said."

Holloway asked:

"Let's consider the evening some fifteen years ago, when you were shown the photographs of you having group sex with two other men. Who were the two men in the photographs?"

"I don't know who they were. I don't remember having sex with them. I was obviously very drunk, and possibly drugged. They certainly weren't in the group I went on holiday with to Estonia."

Holloway continued:

"Staying with the evening when you were shown the photographs. Please name the friend who invited you to his apartment and subsequently introduced you to his two friends."

"That was Jonathan Wheeler. He was about fifteen years older than me and ran a second-hand bookshop somewhere in East London. I haven't seen him for about the last ten years."

Lawson enquired:

"Was it Jonathan Wheeler who initially asked you for 'small favours' to retrieve information from the Ministry of Defence?"

"Yes. He sold second-hand books about military planes and ships and just wanted some technical information about them. He said the information I gave him increased his profit so as a 'thank you' he would give me a small amount of cash. A few years back I was told he had died."

"You say Jonathan Wheeler introduced you to his two associates. Had you seen them before that evening?"

"No."

"Were they the two men who put pressure on you. To use your words, to ruin you if you did not cooperate?"

"Yes."

"What were their names?"

"I was never given their names. That was the only time I met them. They certainly weren't British. They had strong foreign accents. Either then, or perhaps a little later, I assumed they were Russians."

Lawson asked: "Please explain how the contact with your Russian handler was established and how it continued?"

"The two men really frightened me. They gave me a mobile phone and said I would be contacted. I was told not to tell anyone, with the threat if I didn't do what I was told my life wouldn't be worth living. A couple of days later, when I was out by myself, walking in the New Forest I received the promised telephone call. The man told me what he wanted and described how and where to deliver the computer sticks. He told me what payment I would get. I never asked for money. I was very frightened because I felt he was close-by and watching me.

"So, how did the contact continue over the following years?

Archer was hesitant with his reply:

"I never met him personally and was never able to contact him. However, every so often he would telephone me to say what information he wanted."

Lawson commented:

"Let's pull together the sequence of events: you are befriended by a tutor while at Oxford. He introduces you socially to a group of friends who you go on holiday with to Estonia. You have a good time and get drunk on several occasions. One of the friends is Jonathan Wheeler, who owns a second-hand book shop. Later he asks you for 'small favours' to get non-classified information from your place of employment, on military ships and planes, and pays you small amounts of cash as a thank you. He then invites you to his apartment and introduces you to two associates, who you have never seen before. Holiday photographs are handed around. To your horror they are photographs of you involved in group sex with two unknown men. You have no recollection of this event. You are subsequently blackmailed to obtain secret files on defence projects, for which you regularly receive cash payments. And you have continued to do so up until yesterday. Is this a correct assessment?"

Archer begins to sob: "Yes, that's about it."

Holloway asks:

"Please tell us the name and what you know about the Oxford tutor?"

"He's Professor Marcus Longfellow. He was teaching philosophy. I understand he went to teach at a university in America and then retired there about five years ago."

Archer explained that it was Professor Longfellow who arranged and invited him to go on the trip to Estonia. Five or six other students from Oxford also went on the trip, but he could not recall their names. The trip was arranged through one of the socialist organisations Longfellow frequented, and it was an international youth event.

During the next three hours Lawson and Holloway went through the whole affair from Archer's initial recruitment to all the information he had obtained up until yesterday with the hiding of his computer stick under the log. He stated that he was not aware of any other person working at his company being involved in such activity. He made a confession admitting his involvement and signed a written statement, which was taken by Holloway. No promises were made.

Holloway took possession of Archer's company security pass and informed him he was suspended from his employment and must not enter the company premises. He was also forbidden from contacting, or discussing, the case with any of his colleagues.

Archer was made aware that this was the first phase of what would be a long and complex investigation. MI5 would be working on the case in conjunction with the police.

Today a search warrant would be obtained from the Magistrates' Court to search his home address. His computers, iPhone, any relevant electronic equipment and documents would be seized and submitted for forensic and analytical examination. His bank accounts and financial affairs would also be subject to detailed examination.

This interview should be regarded as the first of many. Technical experts would be assigned to undertake detailed examination of his work's computers to assess and identify the systems he had accessed over the years and what secret information he may have illegally downloaded.

The role of MI5 was to gather and analyse the intelligence obtained and, with the relevant military departments, identify the potential consequences Archer's betrayal may have damaged national security. The role of the police was to investigate and collect evidence to support a successful criminal prosecution.

At an early stage of the investigation the police would be liaising with the Crown Prosecution Service to consider how the case should proceed. In the near future, it was likely Archer would formally be arrested. A 'holding charge' would be made to ensure he be remanded in custody to prison pending the undertaking of a detailed and protracted investigation.

Lawson and Holloway returned to MI5 HQ to write up their report. A file on the events would subsequently be prepared and submitted to the police. The likely outcome would be a criminal prosecution for espionage contrary to the Official Secrets Acts 1911 to 1989, with Archer sentenced to a substantial term of imprisonment. The maximum term of imprisonment for Espionage is fourteen years.

Archer's Russian handler having been identified as an FSK intelligence officer, at the Russian Embassy, would be declared persona-non-grata by the British government and expelled.

The interview of Archer had identified further investigations for Lawson and Holloway to undertake. Professor Marcus Longfellow seemed to have been the instigator in the recruitment of Archer. He would be the subject of investigation.

Back at home that evening, Lawson settled down in his favourite comfy chair and reflected on the day's events. In his thoughts, he ran through the long-term effort the Russians had deployed to gain access to the sea-trials data for the UK's latest nuclear submarine. It would, no doubt, be used to develop the technology for their own submarines. Even more important, the data would give them the ability to identify the capabilities of UK submarines and, in times of conflict, assist in analysing their deployment.

He recalled speaking with Director Jane Rigby, when he first joined MI5 and was assigned to her team. As a police officer he had spent his career dealing with general every-day crime and, as he progressed in rank, then dealing with cases of murder and terrorism. He had never encountered cases of espionage. He had naively asked her if espionage was still relevant in today's world?

Jane's polite 'history lesson' response was enlightening:

Since the beginning of time man has coveted his neighbour's property and land. Only a fool believes that does not apply today. England has always been seen as a green and pleasant land. It has been invaded by the Romans; the Normans by William the Conqueror in 1066; and attempts by the Spanish Armada in 1588: the French in 1797 and the Nazi's with Operation Sea Lion in 1940.

Great Britain gained her empire by being the strong aggressor conquering the weak. And so, it continued, with Russia annexing the Crimean Peninsula in 2014 and China currently building islands in the South China Sea to dominate and expand.

Her history lesson had continued:

The UK remains a real target. Russia remains a significant threat, as do other adversaries. During the Cold War, as part of their worldwide military operation, the KGB produced detailed maps of the United Kingdom. Apparently, a dedicated team at the Russian Embassy was deployed to do the work.

As a consequence, the Russians knew the width of our roads, the height of our bridges, the depth of our rivers and the names of our streets. The exact location and purpose of every structure of possible military importance was given. This was in preparation for a potential invasion of our country. It was reported that the Russian military set about mapping the whole world. A mammoth task taking fifty years, which was completed in1997. High-definition satellite surveillance had reduced the time-scale and human effort required to now undertake the task.

The threat to the United Kingdom remains significant. It cannot afford to be weak. That is why the UK's annual defence budget currently stands at $59 billion. China's is $252 billion; Russia is $62 billion and the USA a massive $778 billion. The scale of money devoted annually to military spending is a stark reminder of what a dangerous place the World is.

It was now three years since Lawson posed the question to Jane. Having operated within the intelligence world, he now appreciated the dangers and the need for possessing a strong defence capability. The role of British Intelligence was becoming even more challenging with the added threat from cyber-espionage. The defence and protection of the UK's critical national infrastructure sectors was now a priority.

CHAPTER SEVEN

The Professor and America

Lawson and Holloway attended the conference Silver Room at MI5 HQ for a meeting with Director Jane Rigby. Senior Analyst, Claire, also attended to brief the team on what was now known on the 'Oxford tutor.' He had been identified as Professor Marcus Darius Longfellow with the Faculty of Philosophy, Balliol College, Oxford.

His parents were refuges from Lithuania who came to the United Kingdom, at the end of the Second World War, in 1945. At the beginning of the war Lithuania was occupied by the Soviet Union and then by Nazi Germany. Towards the end of the war the Nazi's retreated with the Soviet Union re-establishing control. Many fled the harsh regime and sought refuge in other countries. In Lithuania, Marcus's father had been an academic. The parents settled in London and changed their family name to Longfellow.

Marcus was their first child, born in August 1946. His main schooling came from his father. He was considered a bright and industrious child who, from an early age, took an interest in politics. Although he was British from birth, he maintained a close affinity with family members still in Lithuania. In 1965 he enrolled as a student at the London School of Economics.

This was a time of student unrest in universities across Europe and the USA. The LSE became strongly associated with the student rebellion. Marcus Longfellow was identified as a radical student, often at the forefront of demonstrations. He appeared often on police Special Branch reports but was never charged, nor convicted, for any criminal offence.

Having obtained his first university degree, he continued studying in the academic environment eventually becoming a university lecturer. He continued to be active in political and anti-war demonstrations and was monitored attending communist supporting organisations.

In 1978, when a tutor at Balliol College, he arranged to take a group of students to Cuba to the World Festival of Youths and Students, organised by the Young Communist League. In 1985 he took a group to the event when it was held in Moscow. The events were actively supported and financed by the Soviet Communist Party.

Over the years his actions resulted in further monitoring by the police and security services, but no criminal activity was ever established. He was believed to have left the UK in about 1990 to seek teaching posts in America. He had retained British citizenship and was known to return infrequently to the UK. Research had identified he was now retired and living somewhere in Florida.

Claire's research had identified that between 1982 and 1985 one of the students at Balliol College, who had received tuition from Longfellow, was sitting Conservative Member of Parliament, Timothy Risborough, known as 'Tim.' MI5 had contacted him hoping to arrange a visit to his parliamentary office. He had declined, insisting any visit would be to his home address. Holloway was assigned to undertake the visit.

Mark Holloway drove up from London to meet MP Tim Risborough at his home on the outskirts of Cheltenham in the county of Gloucester. The large modern detached house, within several acres of land, was situated at the end of a long driveway. Parked near the house was a silver-coloured Aston Martin car.

As he walked to the main entrance door of the house, Holloway gave the car an admiring glance noting it was a DB11 worth in excess of £100,000. Tim Risborough opened the door and greeted him with enthusiasm, clasping Holloway's outstretched right hand with both hands and almost pulling him into the house.

"Welcome to my home Mark. May I call you Mark? I've been looking forward to your visit and somewhat intrigued to know what it's about."

Further pleasantries were exchanged. Holloway was taken to the well-furnished ground floor study and invited to sit on a burgundy-coloured, leather chesterfield sofa. Risborough sat on a swivel chair next to a large oak desk and turned the chair, so he was facing Holloway. The walls of the study displayed numerous framed photographs, mainly of Risborough standing with various national and international dignitaries. Holloway noted the current and two former British prime ministers in the collection, and on his desk a framed photograph of Risborough being presented to Her Majesty the Queen.

Risborough poured himself a large whisky. Holloway declined the offer and politely asked for a coffee, which Risborough's attractive younger wife delivered. From the outset, Holloway identified Risborough as a flamboyant, yet pleasant and likeable character.

"Mark, I hope you didn't mind visiting me at home. I declined your earlier request to meet me in my parliamentary office. I couldn't have MI5 snooping around there. That would have had tongues wagging with my staff thinking I was a spy." He gave a mischievous smile.

Holloway asked that the content of their meeting should remain confidential. He explained they were looking into the background of one of his tutors from Risborough's time as a student at Balliol College, Oxford, the tutor being Professor Marcus Longfellow from the Faculty of Philosophy.

Holloway was careful with his explanation. He simply said some concern had been raised about the tutor's alleged association with a foreign intelligence agency. Risborough confirmed he was a student at Balliol College from 1982 to 1985 and received tuition from Longfellow.

Risborough was asked to give his recollections of Longfellow and responded:

"His nickname was 'Einstein's brother' because he reminded the students of Albert Einstein with his greying unkempt spiky hair. He always dressed the same: a multicoloured polka dot bow tie, check shirt and a tartan waistcoat which was always unbuttoned. All the colours clashed. And invariably he would smoke a foul-smelling Sherlock Holmes-style pipe. He didn't have a car and would cycle around Oxford on a lady's bike with a wicker basket on the front. I have this hilarious picture in my mind of him cycling furiously into the quadrangle, late for one of his tutorials, with his basket full of groceries." He added with an element of sarcasm: "His lunchtime tutorials were a treat to be missed. He would pour the students a glass of cheap Sherry, then hand round a bowl of potato crisps."

Holloway asked: "Was he married?"

"No, and I couldn't imagine him having a girlfriend."

Holloway asked: "You paint a very colourful picture of him. How did you view him?"

"He was an eccentric, but I believe he enjoyed that characterisation and I wondered how much of that was a deliberate act. He was extremely intelligent and, quietly, very shrewd."

"How did you view his politics?"

"He was left-wing without much doubt. I always got the impression his heart wasn't in teaching. He saw it as a soft option. The college gave him a salary and a cosy place to live. He enjoyed the social side of things mixing with the young students. To be honest, I didn't learn a useful thing from his lectures."

Holloway enquired: "How did he express or show his left-wing views."

Risborough replied: "In almost everything. He constantly rubbished government policy and would frequently go on protest marches, particularly if it involved anything against the USA. At the time I was there I remember him organising buses to take groups of his students to Greenham Common and London to protest about nuclear weapons, and the American's storing their cruise missiles over here."

Holloway asked: "Did he indicate his views on Communism?"

"Yes, and very actively. He used to encourage his favoured students to go with him to weekend events. He was a supporter of the Young Communist League and would talk about attending the World Festival of Youths and Students in Cuba, organised by the Young Communist League. I think that was in about 1978. In my last year at Oxford, he was recruiting students to attend the next World Festival of Youths and Students to be held in Moscow. That would have been in 1985. He tried to persuade me to go."

Holloway asked: "Did you go?"

Risborough replied: "No. My late father, who was a QC and did legal work for the government, was adamant I shouldn't get involved. He said the organisation was an outlet for Soviet propaganda."

"Did you attend any of the social events, or day trips, organised by Longfellow?"

"No, not one. My late father would joke that Longfellow was probably head hunting for the Russians."

"Did you ever see Longfellow once you completed your degree?"

"No. I recall being told he had packed his bags and gone off to America to teach, which I thought ironic since he was anti-USA. It was also a little ironic, that Longfellow having failed to interest me in being a Russian spy, the British then attempt to recruit me as a spy."

"Please explain your last comment?"

"Having obtain my First-Class Honours degree I entered, and was successful, in the Civil Service Fast Track programme for graduates. When the list is published, the various government departments race to select the best new graduates. I was invited to a protracted interview at the Foreign and Commonwealth Office. At the end of the process the rather pompous chairman then said he was actually a director with the Secret Intelligent Service. I obviously looked puzzled, because he added: 'in the media we are more commonly known as MI6.' He said they would like to consider me to join them."

Risborough then explained to Holloway he was then given a lecture on how he mustn't tell anyone about the content of the interview. He was further told it must remain confidential about him being considered as an applicant and what the position and training would entail. Holloway enquired what was his response.

"It wasn't a career choice for me. I can't keep secrets. By the end of the day, I would have told all my mates." He said this with a broad grin.

Holloway made a light-hearted comment:

"Well, at least you have a James Bond Aston Martin."

Risborough laughed: "I couldn't have afforded my beauty Aston on an MI6 salary."

He went on to explain he briefly took up a position with the Home Office, but quickly decided the Civil Service was not for him. With the assistance of his late father, he qualified as a barrister but then he'd became involved in politics. At the age of thirty years, he became a Conservative Member of Parliament. In response to a question posed by Holloway he confirmed that he did not know Steven Archer.

The meeting was concluded. Despite his earlier light-hearted comment that he could not keep a secret, Risborough assured Holloway their conversation would remain private and confidential. Holloway reported back to Director Jane Rigby and Lawson on the outcome of his meeting with the colourful MP Tim Risborough.

A decision was reached whereby MI5 would liaise with the FBI to establish the current whereabouts of Professor Marcus Longfellow, who was believed to be living in America. The United Kingdom has, what is often described as, a 'special relationship' with the United States of America in relation to the sharing of intelligence and security matters. This can be traced back to informal secret meetings held during the Second World War.

Lawson prepared a report on the Longfellow investigation, which was given a classification marked Secret. Through established protocols, the report was delivered to the FBI (Federal Bureau of Investigation). He was subsequently invited to the American Embassy in London to discuss the matter.

The recently opened new American Embassy is located in Nine Elms, Battersea and overlooks the River

Thames. It is the largest American embassy in Western Europe. FBI special agents operating in foreign countries from USA embassies are referred to as legal attaches. The team working out of the embassy in London maintain close liaison with UK law enforcement and security services.

Two weeks on from submitting his report, Lawson attended the American Embassy in London. The feedback was encouraging. The current address of Longfellow had been identified as being in Florida. He was now retired but had previously spent several years teaching at several different American universities. The FBI had spoken with Longfellow. He would not be returning to the UK but had indicated he was prepared to be interviewed by MI5 at his Florida home. The FBI in America were keen to pursue enquires and have face-to-face liaison with MI5. Authority was approved for such meetings to proceed.

Back at MI5 HQ, agreement was reached that Lawson would undertake the trip. The Finance Department having stipulated it did not warrant the expense, nor operational need, to send a second officer!

Lawson arrived late evening at RAF Brize Norton, located in the county of Oxfordshire seventy-five miles northwest of London. It's the largest RAF station in the UK. He had 'hitched a lift' on a military transport aircraft. He booked into the Officers' quarters for a brief overnight sleep, as the flight departure was scheduled for 04:00 hours.

The aircraft was taking a company of Special Forces soldiers, on a six-month deployment for jungle warfare training, to the British Army Training Support Unit in Belize. The aircraft's scheduled refuelling stop, after an eight-hour flight, was the John F. Kennedy International Airport, New York. It was here that Lawson, along with several other passengers from the diplomatic service, would disembark.

The flight would then continue on to Belize, which is on the eastern coast of Central America, bordered on the north by Mexico. The flight went without incident, although Lawson was surprised to see that the soldiers retained their rifles in their possession during the flight.

Having disembarked at JFK, Lawson took an internal flight, for the two-hundred-mile journey, to the Ronald Reagan Washington International Airport. On arrival, and once through customs and passport control, he sat down in the arrival lounge to await collection where he was to be taken to the British Embassy. It was then 10:00 hours American time. With the six-hour time difference, and the 04:00 hours British time departure, he had been travelling for over twelve hours.

He was feeling tired and a little disoriented. He was almost asleep and made no connection with the repeated tannoy announcements. Suddenly, he woke with a start having received a gentle shake on his shoulder. Looking up, standing in front of him was a man in full chauffeur uniform:

"Sir, are you Mr Lawson?"

Lawson thought for a moment, and with a sheepish response:

"Yes. Sorry I must have fallen asleep."

In reality, in his disoriented state, he had gone back to being Ben Swan. Faux pas number one. There would be others!

He was driven to the British Embassy in a smart Jaguar motor car. Now he was awake, and back in 'Julian Lawson mode' he enjoyed a light-hearted conversation with the British chauffeur, who joked that he had tried to get him the Ambassador's Bentley. The chauffeur, Brian, explained he was ex-military and had undertaken Advanced Enhanced Driver Training.

Lawson's visit to the British Embassy, located in the plush Massachusetts Avenue, was brief. It was part of the protocol and courtesy, for HM government personnel, to make contact when working in the USA. The same chauffeur then drove him to the hotel.

Lawson was to spend a two-night stay at the Four Seasons Hotel, Georgetown. Shortly after arrival at the hotel, he made contact with his FBI liaison officer and was collected and driven to FBI Head Quarters.

The FBI HQ is named after its first director. The J. Edgar Hoover Building is located along Pennsylvania Avenue, Washington DC. It is a massive structure; an eight-story building with three underground parking garages. The architectural style is known as Brutalism. It is the main HQ for FBI World operations. His liaison officer introduced him to colleagues and then, after a light lunch, gave him a tour of the complex.

He was surprised to note the building was open to the public for tours. Obviously, certain secure and sensitive areas remained out of bounds. That day Lawson walked the three miles back to his hotel. It was a pleasant evening. He enjoyed the stroll along Pennsylvania Avenue, observing other famous buildings including the United States Capitol Building, the meeting place of the United States Congress.

Next morning, he walked from his hotel back to FBI HQ, taking a slight detour to view the most famous address in America: 1600 Pennsylvania Avenue, the address of the White House. He was met at FBI HQ by his liaison officer, Special Agent Jeff Goldsmith, and taken to meet his colleagues for an early morning coffee.

There were about twelve FBI agents in the large open plan office. All with their jackets off and sporting shoulder holsters with handguns. They appeared to be a friendly group all referring to each other by their first names. Lawson was there to have a meeting with one of the directors again, partly as a formality to receive authority to undertake the interview with Professor Longfellow, and to receive any up-date the FBI may have.

While Lawson was still with some of the group drinking coffee, another agent walked across:

"Guys, Wadey is now ready to see Julian."

Lawson was taken into the director's office. The meeting lasted about twenty minutes. The director reported that their records showed Longfellow had entered the United States in June of 1995. He had been employed for short periods of time as a tutor at various universities. During the first year of his stay in America, on two occasions he was on record as having joined anti-war demonstrations outside the White House. His conduct was described as 'vocal and aggressive.' This resulted in him being warned that a repeat would see his work permit revoked and, thus, jeopardise his continued presence in the USA.

Nothing further was recorded to Longfellow's detriment on either police or FBI files. The universities where he had taught in America had been identified and, as a consequence of the intelligence on him received from MI5, the FBI would now seek to interview him. Lawson thanked Wadey for seeing him.

On leaving his office, Lawson noted the sign on the director's door: Director James WADEY. Lawson was embarrassed.

He turned to address Jeff:

"Christ, how embarrassing. Throughout our meeting I repeatedly called him Wadey. You were all calling each other by your first names, so I assumed it was his first name. I now see it is his surname."

One of the other agents responded:

"We don't like him, so we just refer to him as Wadey. Don't worry, Julian. He'll just think you're from one of those posh English boarding schools we see in films where all the pupils are called by their surnames."

Lawson still felt embarrassed. Faux pas number two!

Lawson was scheduled to fly down to Florida first thing the following morning. With the afternoon free, Special Agent Jeff Goldsmith suggested he take him on a tour of the Quantico FBI Academy, which he readily accepted.

Cars seized by the FBI, usually from drug dealers, are often retained and used as their service transport. The car chosen for the visit to Quantico was a Porsche

911 sports car, with Jeff commenting that the department only retained the 'quality vehicles.'

Quantico is the FBI national law enforcement training facility and research centre, located in five hundred and seventy acres of woodland in Virginia, thirty-six miles outside of Washington DC. It is an extremely impressive and well-equipped establishment undertaking a multitude of courses. Lawson was taken on a three-hour tour of the complex, including the firing range, to watch SWAT teams in training and to the impressive Hogan's Alley.

Hogan's Alley is a training complex simulating a small town, built with the help of Hollywood set designers. It gives realistic training to agents, who are confronted with stressful armed incidents where firearms are deployed. Lawson was surprised to note that even when in the classroom environment instructors retain their holstered firearms.

The FBI requirement for an agent to attend Quantico is between the age of twenty-three to thirty-seven years of age, must be a citizen of the United States with the minimum education qualification of a bachelor's degree. The academy also trains senior police leaders from across the World.

Next morning Lawson took a two-and-a-half-hour flight from Washington DC to Fort Lauderdale-Hollywood International Airport. He was met by Cheryl Lockyer from the Miami FBI office. She was a delightful blonde, confident, 'all American' lady. He thought to himself, with a degree of mischief: 'They've obviously sent the most attractive girl in the office to impress the Limey James Bond secret agent.'

It was a thirty-minute drive to Miami. Cheryl suggested she take Lawson for a sea-food lunch at an open-air restaurant on the route back. As is the acknowledged policy with all intelligence personnel, when in a public place like a restaurant, business is not discussed. Their lunch-time conversation centred around the flight and the local sights.

On reaching the Miami FBI building, Cheryl took Lawson into the large open plan main office. Similar to FBI HQ in Washington, all staff were in shirtsleeves and carrying shoulder holstered firearms. She introduced him to the team:

"This is our British visitor. Julian, get to know the team over a coffee. When you're ready, call into my office to talk business."

Cheryl walked across the room and into her office. Lawson looked at the signage on the door: 'Cheryl Lockyer, Bureau Chief Miami.' She was the Boss. Faux pas number three!

Later that afternoon Lawson held a meeting with Cheryl. She was in possession of the classified MI5 report on Longfellow, which she had received two weeks ago. Her bureau office had undertaken local research. Florida state has a population of over twenty-one million. There are over fifty registered universities and colleges for higher degree level education. Some are state funded and others privately. There is no central register to identify the names of academic staff employed at the various institutions.

Longfellow's last known full-time employment was some ten years earlier at a state funded college. The college records on his employment were limited. He was there for two years teaching philosophy and there was nothing recorded to his detriment. No current member of staff had any personal knowledge of him.

The FBI Miami bureau is taking an interest in Longfellow, because of the MI5 intelligence reports about his association with Russian contacts whilst a tutor at Oxford. They were particularly interested to note that in 1975 he visited Cuba to attend the World Festival of Youths and Students organised by the Young Communist League, and again in 1985 when it was held in Moscow.

The island of Cuba is located south of the state of Florida. In 1959 communist rule was established following the revolution led by Fidel Castro. The Republic of Cuba was then governed by the Communist Party of Cuba.

During the Cold War between the Soviet Union and the USA, nuclear war nearly broke out in 1962, when Moscow deployed nuclear cruise missiles on the mainland of Cuba. Soviet troops were stationed there until 1991. Before the collapse of the Soviet Union, the country depended on Moscow for substantial aid.

Cheryl considered it relevant that Longfellow, a British academic with communist sympathies and an apparent hatred for America, attended a Young Communist League festival in Cuba. Then several years later moved, not just to America, but to Florida with Cuba on its doorstep. Florida now has a large population of Cuban refugees. The FBI is aware that some of the 'refugees' are not what they appear to be and actively support the Communist regime.

Longfellow had said he will meet with the MI5 representative at his home in Naples, a town with a population of twenty-thousand. The town is located on the west coast of Florida facing the Gulf of Mexico. He won't cooperate if an FBI representative is present. Cheryl has agreed for Lawson to meet with Longfellow alone. The FBI will arrange their meeting with him at a later date. The FBI office telephoned Longfellow to make the arrangement for Lawson to visit him the next day.

Lawson was driven back to Fort Lauderdale where arrangements had been made for him to stay at the Holiday Inn Hotel. He enquired at Reception about hiring a car for the following day. The helpful Concierge made the necessary arrangements.

At 09:00 hours the next morning a silver-coloured Ford Mustang Convertible was parked outside the hotel waiting for Lawson. The ever-helpful Concierge handed him the keys, plus gave verbal instructions on use of the car, together with a map and tips on travelling to Naples on Route 75.

It is an eighty-mile journey across the Everglades, an incredibly remote part of Florida. The route westward to the Gulf of Mexico is famously known as Alligator Alley. Lawson took the advice of the Concierge and drove several laps around the vast hotel car park to familiarise himself with the controls of the Mustang with its automatic gear shift.

Then with the car radio switched on and tuned into a Country music radio station he was off driving towards Alligator Alley. It was a bright warm sunny morning. Lawson felt relaxed and happy, wondering how he was going to convince Mark Holloway the trip had been hard work.

At the halfway point, about forty miles into the journey, he took a slight detour and followed the signposts to a place to pull-in with a parked refreshment trailer.

He purchased a bottle of cold drink and walked towards the shimmering water of the Everglades. It was a primeval wilderness, as if stepping back into another world. In front of him he saw an exceptionally large alligator that appeared to be sleeping in the warm sun. A prehistoric frightening, yet magnificent reptile.

Lawson took out his iPhone and took two quick photographs. The alligator appeared to take exception to having his photograph taken. His movement was swift, as was Lawson who rapidly stepped back several paces. He turned and realised several other equally large alligators were nearby.

He remembered the Concierge's words of advice not to stray from the refreshment trailer. Safely, back at the trailer, with a sense of black-humour he thought about what would have happened if he had been killed by an alligator. MI5 HQ would have ensured he was described in the Press as a 'foolish tourist.' Then a high-level debate would have taken place to decide whether he was killed on active service and, thus, qualified to have his name inscribed on the Roll of Honour plaque discreetly displayed within the inner sanctum.

The service does not do public announcements on the death of an officer. Lawson recalled the death of a

colleague two years earlier whilst on a terrorist operation in the Highlands of Scotland. A member of his
team had been shot dead. Even in death Lawson did not
know his colleague's true identity and, thus, was unable to speak to, or visit, his family to offer condolences.
Sometimes it is a harsh and seemingly uncaring world.

Lawson continued his drive, back on Route 75, west
towards Naples. Using the car's Satnav, he navigated
his way direct to Longfellow's address in the town of
Naples. It was a two-bedroom ground-floor condomin-
ium situated within a gated private country club community. Longfellow lived alone.

He opened the door wearing a multi-coloured
Hawaiian shirt with matching knee length shorts, and
bare feet. The leathery appearance of his skin suggested
damage caused by too much exposure to the sun. He
was extremely thin and looked older than his years.

He was polite but did not appear over pleased to see
Lawson. Longfellow invited him to sit on a wicker chair
on the shaded side of the balcony facing a lush green
golf course. He acknowledged that he did not play golf.
Lawson observed several communal golf carts slowly
driving on the private roads within the complex, which
was clearly the preserve of the retired. Longfellow did
not attempt to offer any refreshment. From the outset,
Lawson sensed he was a lonely man.

Lawson formally introduced himself and explained
the role of MI5. Longfellow agreed the interview could
be recorded. Lawson placed a mini digital voice recorder
on the low table in front of them and switched it onto
active mode. He explained MI5 had received verifiable

information that the Russian intelligence service had run an active covert operation to steal UK government military secrets using British nationals. Longfellow did not comment and almost looked disinterested.

Lawson opened his laptop computer and, referring to the content on the screen, ran through a resume of Longfellow's history. Longfellow confirmed it was correct.

He acknowledged his three years as an undergraduate at the London School of Economics. He had no objection to being referred to as an active and disruptive student involved in anti-war demonstrations. He was happy, almost proud, to accept his sympathies were to the Communist cause.

Likewise, he freely acknowledged he had arranged for some of his students to attend the World Festival of Youths and Students, organised by the Young Communist League, in Cuba in 1975 and, again, when it was held in Moscow in 1985. He confirmed he had attended both events. He saw no problem that the Young Communist League was sponsored from Moscow. He further acknowledged he was a pacifist.

He explained that in the nineteen-sixties he felt there was a dangerous imbalance in technology and science between the USA and the Soviet Union, the imbalance being in favour of the USA. He considered the World would be a safer place if the power were equal.

He denied ever knowingly giving information to any person acting for the Soviet government. From memory, perhaps from newspaper reports, he had an awareness that during the sixties and seventies some

British academics may have given secrets to Soviet officials to lessen the imbalance.

His memory was vague, but possibly secrets to do with the development of nuclear weapons. He was sure it was not a case of 'meeting a KGB agent at some remote location and handing over a file of secrets.' No, it was more likely to have been a group of British academic scientists working on a subject, meeting a team of Soviet academic scientists working on a similar project and, perhaps one individual, deciding to share their findings.

If it helped level the imbalance, he considered it justified. Illogical, but that was his view. He had not been involved in any such exchange and could not put a name to anyone who had.

He considered himself a lifelong socialist. He had been a member of the Socialist Workers' Party of Britain and had written articles for the weekly left-wing newspaper, the Socialist Worker. Longfellow saw the emergence of the Soviet Union as the world's first socialist state. And, yes, he had attended numerous socialist meetings and events in the UK and, by invitation, in former Soviet countries. However, he denied ever being approached to spy for them in the UK.

Longfellow was clearly showing annoyance with Lawson's constant line of questioning. What was the point?

He had acknowledged he was a lifelong socialist, had admired the former Soviet Union, but had never been involved in any spying activity for a foreign country. Adding, with a cynical smile, that he had never possessed any secrets to give. Lawson, having established Longfellow's background, then focused on the specific allegations.

"The period I wish to concentrate on is your time at Balliol College, Oxford between 1981 to 1985 when you were teaching philosophy. During this period, were you actively involved with the Socialist Workers' Party of Britain and with the Socialist Workers Student Society?"

"Yes, yes to both parts. Get on with your questions."

"And during this period, through your association with socialist organisations, were you meeting like-minded people from countries in the Soviet Block."

"Yes. Yes, next question Mr Lawson."

"The allegation is that you were actively involved in identifying students with sympathies to socialism and the Soviet cause."

"Identifying students for what?" Longfellow asked, in a mood of annoyance.

"Identifying 'bright' students with socialist leanings who, in the future, might hold important positions in government or industry. Such students would eventually be recruited by the KGB and, later in their professional career, be in a senior position to obtain secrets of use to the Soviet Union."

"That is rubbish Mr Lawson. Your people have got it wrong."

Lawson remained patient:

"Please explain your interpretation of what you were doing and why?"

"It was nothing to do with identifying a student as a potential spy. I am a committed Socialist. My hatred is for the British class system, and the unfair privilege that comes with it. That is well known. My recruitment, as you refer to it, would be to help a promising student in his social development. I would introduce him to socialist groups, often with links to the Labour Party. For me success would be to see one of my students, in later years, as a trade union official or even as a Labour Member of Parliament."

Lawson continued:

"Let us discuss the trips abroad that you arranged. In about 1984, did you arrange a student group holiday to Estonia."

"Yes, it was organised by the International Young Communist League."

"Did your group join up with students from other countries?"

"Naturally. It was an international event."

"How was the trip funded?"

Longfellow replied:

"With most trips, our UK branch would assist with the cost of travel, and the host country would pay for accommodation and food."

"And was it normal for the host country to hold evening gatherings where alcohol was consumed?"

"Yes."

"Have you ever been drunk, Marcus?"

He nodded and smiled: "Often."

"Do you recall getting drunk on the Estonian trip?"

"Probably, but I can't recall."

"Do you recall members of your student group getting drunk?"

"Again, I cannot recall but most likely. They were young men away from home having a good time."

Lawson said: "One of your students on the Estonian trip was Steven Archer. Do you remember him going on the trip?"

"No. To be honest, I have no recollection of a student called Steven Archer. I don't believe I can remember the name of any of the students. They just passed through the college and through my mind."

"The allegation is that at a drunken party he had sex with two other men."

Longfellow interrupted: "That is not a crime."

"Please let me continue. Did drunken parties sometimes involve sex?"

"Again, Mr Lawson, young men all over the world get drunk and sometimes enjoy themselves having sex."

"The allegation is that Mr Archer was too drunk to know what was happening. Colour photographs of the act were taken and later used to blackmail him."

Longfellow responded:

"I was not aware of this particular act nor about such an act being photographed."

"Do you recall a Jonathan Wheeler?"

"Would that be Jonathan Wheeler, who owned a second-hand bookshop?"

"Yes. What can you tell me about him, and did he go on the Estonian trip?"

"I knew him through my association with the Socialist Workers Party and do believe he was on the trip. We did not have a personal friendship. I cannot tell you anything more about him."

Lawson continued with the questioning:

"Mr Archer states, at a later date that he was invited to Jonathan Wheeler's London apartment. Two other unknown men were present. During the course of the evening, the Estonian trip was mentioned, and holiday photographs were produced. To the horror of Mr Archer, the photographs include some of him having sex with two other unknown men. He was then blackmailed to obtain classified UK secrets. I am not going to go into details of what the secrets were. What do you know of the events at Jonathan Wheeler's apartment?"

"Nothing whatever. I was not there, and no one has ever mentioned it to me."

Lawson sat back in his chair, looked directly at Longfellow and spoke slowly:

"You're an intelligent man Professor Longfellow. When you arranged, and took young students to events in communist counties as you did to Cuba, Russia (Moscow) and Estonia did you not consider the dangers?"

Longfellow interrupted: "Dangers? What dangers?"

Lawson continued: "The dangers of them being exploited and recruited by intelligence agencies."

"No, I did not. I view these countries and regimes differently to you. Have you, for example, ever studied Cuba?"

"No" replied Lawson.

"You should."

"What is the point you are making?" asked Lawson.

For the first time during the interview, Longfellow became animated:

"By the late nineteen-fifties Havana was then what Las Vegas had become. It was the playground for rich Americans with its gambling and prostitution. The poor were exploited and had to fend for themselves. After the revolution, the Communist Party of Cuba came into government. It eradicated hunger and poverty, introduced free good health care and education. Whether you are a doctor or road-sweeper you all became equal and were given respect. That was my idea of socialism."

"On reflection, and with no disrespect intended, do you feel you were 'used' by KGB officers to unwittingly assist in identifying potential recruits?"

"That's for your people to decide. It was a long time ago, and I do not intend to worry about it."

Preparing to leave Lawson commented:

"This is very pleasant. Are you enjoying living here?"

"Yes. I intend to remain here in my retirement. I might occasionally visit the UK, but my life is here."

Longfellow confirmed he was now fully retired. He had not undertaken any paid employment for the previous eight years. He rarely visited Miami, or any other town, and did not involve himself with any political organisation. Since living in America, he had not visited Cuba.

Lawson stood up, looked out from the balcony onto the golf course and commented:

"May I make an observation? You're a lifelong socialist, with support for communist ideals, and with an active dislike for America. Yet you end up living in a luxury gated community in the USA."

Longfellow smiled:

"Would you prefer to have me living in a small apartment in a cold Moscow? Earlier you mentioned I was intelligent. Perhaps that's why I made a decision to live in a warm sunny climate. I do not think the residents realise it, but this place is an ideal socialist community. All the amenities are shared: the restaurants, the gym, the health facilities and even our transport is shared with the communal golf carts. It's all managed by a 'collective' residents' committee. Reminds me of a perfect Socialist Cuba."

Lawson picked up his digital voice recorder from the low-table and held it in his hand. Before switching the machine off he showed it to Longfellow and commented:

"This is an amazing piece of equipment. Not only is the clarity perfect, but it also has other functions. Note the small flashing red light and the direction arrow. It tells me there is a second recording system nearby, in the direction of the vase on your bookcase. May I examine it?"

He moved towards the vase and removed from the inside a small dictaphone. Longfellow looked embarrassed but did not speak.

Lawson examined it and held it towards Longfellow:

"Is this yours?"

"Yes."

"Why?"

"I mentioned your visit to a retired lawyer friend within the community and he recommended I record your visit."

Lawson examined the dictaphone. It was a cheap commercial machine. He satisfied himself it was not the professional type one would expect from a foreign intelligence agency. He handed it to Longfellow, making no further comment.

Back to Fort Lauderdale on Route 75. Although he had undertaken a long interview with Longfellow without being offered any refreshment, he decided to drive the eighty-mile return journey without stopping at the half-way point for a drink at the refreshment trailer. His previous close call with the alligator was possibly an incentive not to stop.

On reaching the hotel he, reluctantly, handed the keys of the Ford Mustang back to the Concierge. Lawson had enjoyed the experience of driving a powerful convertible Ford Mustang through the wilderness of the American Everglades.

Next morning Lawson made a visit to the FBI office in Miami to brief Cheryl Lockyer on his interview with Professor Marcus Longfellow:

Longfellow was proud to be known as a lifelong socialist and, in the past, an active supporter of communism. He acknowledged, as a university tutor, that he was keen to encourage students in the direction of socialism. He associated with like-minded people, including those from Soviet Bloc countries, and took students abroad to communist organised events.

There was no evidence to indicate Longfellow ever gave away secrets and, he actually commented, he never had possession of any to give. Certainly, his conduct would have assisted the KGB in their recruitment. The question remains, was he knowingly part of the process to blackmail and recruit students to spy, or just a naïve idealist who failed to realise he was being used by the KGB? On the current evidence, Lawson favoured the latter, but would keep his options open pending any further intelligence which might come to light.

Lawson's Miami hosts arranged for him to be taken to the airport for his flight to Washington DC, then another to New York where he was scheduled, once again, to use the services of the RAF to 'hitch a lift' on a military transport plane flying back to RAF Brize Norton, England.

Chapter Eight

Operation Dragonfly

His plans were to change dramatically when he landed at Ronald Reagan Washington International Airport. At Passport Control, he opened his passport and presented it at the desk, expecting to be waved through. There appeared to be a problem. He was escorted to a holding-room and told someone would be with him shortly. Lawson wondered what the problem could be. Was it the change of name? Some three years earlier he had travelled to Washington using his birth name, and passport, Ben Swan. Had the facial recognition cameras identified the fact Ben Swan was now calling himself Julian Lawson? He would have some explaining to do.

Twenty minutes passed. The door opened:

"Good morning Sir, I've come to deliver you to the British Embassy."

Standing in the doorway was Brian, the chauffeur from the embassy.

Lawson looked surprised:

"What's going on, I was expecting to take a direct flight to New York. There was no mention of calling at the embassy?"

"I don't know the reason, Sir. Apparently, it was a last-minute request."

He smiled and added: "Sorry, but I still haven't been able to get you the Ambassador's Bentley."

Arriving at the British Embassy he was taken to a small conference room and introduced to an MI5 liaison officer attached to the embassy. Lawson had met him once before when he previously called there on his way to Florida. Coffee was served.

The liaison officer spoke:

"There's hell of a lot of urgent legal negotiations going on at present. I hope you haven't made plans to be home tomorrow. A new urgent 'high grade' assignment is being put together. I won't say more for the present and wait until the Chief arrives."

Lawson and the liaison officer poured out more coffee and sat quietly waiting.

After about twenty minutes a team of five men entered the conference room and immediately took their seats. There was no time for formal introductions. The man seated at the head of the table was clearly 'The Chief' and was referred to as Christopher. A noticeably confident, well-groomed individual who spoke with an upper-class English accent.

"Gentlemen, time is of the essence. I will only give you a basic overview because, for the present, that is all I have. This will be a joint operation with FBI and MI5, with appropriate government and military involvement as further intelligence is received. The strategy is being developed at a fast pace. The joint operation has been designated as Operation Dragonfly."

Charles poured himself a coffee and continued:

"So, what is currently known? Recent Intelligence, from a sensitive source, has been intercepted to indicate that an assassination is being planned for three to four days hence. Unfortunately, currently the identity of the target is not known. Identity of assassin not known. The rationale for the killing is not known and nor is the method of killing known."

He stopped, flipped open his iPad which was on the desk in front of him and continued:

"It is suggested that the killing will take place in mid-Atlantic." After a pause, he added: "On board the ocean liner, Queen Mary 2, Flagship of the Cunard Line."

Charles explained, with the limited intelligence currently available, there was insufficient to make an arrest or to successfully disrupt the killing. Likewise, with about four-thousand passengers and crew on board, it was not a feasible proposition to cancel or delay the ship from sailing.

QM2 will depart New York Brooklyn Cruise Terminal at 17:00 hours today. The Check-in opens at 13:00 hours and closes at15:45 hours. It is scheduled as an eight-night cruise to Southampton, England arriving at 06:30 hours.

Charles commented:

"The intelligence is currently slim but, such is the quality of the sensitive source, we cannot ignore it. We must put human resources in place now. As the intelligence is developed, and we gain more detail and clarification, decisions will be taken to either abort or escalate."

He explained that, in addition to preparing an operational strategy, complex legal negotiations were in progress. Jurisdiction was a tricky issue requiring international negotiations. The ship was registered in Bermuda but owned by Carnival Corporation registered in Panama. The military and law enforcement agencies of America and Britain would also be involved.

The agreed strategy was to embed two FBI agents and two MI5 officers on board as passengers, with an additional FBI team posing as crew. The ship's captain and his chief security officer had been briefed and were fully supportive of the proposed action.

A significant team was being established at FBI HQ to undertake extensive research. At this time, it was not known if the alleged assassins would travel as passengers or crew. It was imperative that additional information was forthcoming without delay to reduce the pool of possible assassins and to identify the target. The ship would have on board 2,691 passengers holding passports from eleven countries, and 1,292 officers and crew emanating from more than ten countries.

Looking across the conference table to Lawson, Charles addressed him:

"Julian, no doubt you are wondering why your journey home was interrupted, or you may have guessed.

You will be one of the MI5 team being deployed onto QM2 as a passenger. Your partner for the trip is currently in the US and making her way to New York."

Lawson noted, he was to have a partner and it was a lady. He made no comment and just nodded, and inwardly smiled.

Charles added:

"It's a ninety-minute flight to New York. Priority clearance has been arranged to facilitate your journey to FBI HQ New York. Further details to follow. You will embark the ship, as a passenger, with your current identity."

Lawson departed the meeting, with the MI5 liaison officer who accompanied him to the airport. With his contacts, the liaison officer ensured priority clearance through Customs and onto the aircraft. On arrival at New York Airport, he was met by another liaison officer and swiftly taken to the FBI HQ.

He immediately joined a meeting convened to discuss Operation Dragonfly. It was a fast-moving investigation with further details forthcoming since he'd left Washington. The latest intelligence stated that the killers were either American or British passport holders posing as husband and wife. Their identities remained unknown.

The source information indicated a handgun with a silencer would be used to kill the target. The gun had been smuggled on board during an earlier cruise. It was indicated that following the killing, which would be undertaken discreetly during the hours of darkness, the body would be thrown overboard. The killing would be undertaken when the ship was cruising in mid-Atlantic on the third or fourth day at sea. There was still no additional intelligence to assist with the identification of the target.

In view of the latest intelligence, the operation would proceed with Lawson and his 'partner' boarding the ship posing as passengers. Two FBI agents would embark together posing as passengers. Four FBI agents would also join the ship posing as crew.

Time was getting short. QM2 was berthed at the Brooklyn Cruise Terminal, which is twelve miles from the New York FBI HQ. He was handed, in a Cunard plastic wallet, the necessary passenger tickets and boarding passes which he placed in his shoulder bag. His 'partner' would meet up with him in the departure lounge. He would be able to identify her by her distinctive red coloured shoulder bag, with a small Union flag patch, and she would be standing under the main clock.

Lawson was driven to the Brooklyn Cruise Terminal and dropped off. Carrying a suitcase and a backpack he walked slowly through the open entrance and into the departure lounge. His unknown 'partner' with her distinctive red shoulder bag was quickly seen standing under the main clock. He was feeling somewhat apprehensive, with the thought of meeting up with an unknown woman, and immediately expected to pose as partners.

She had her back to him. She was slim with long blonde hair tied in a ponytail. He then realised, in the rush, he had not been given her name. Lawson walked up behind her and hesitated:

"Good afternoon, are you…?"

He stopped in mid-sentence as she turned to face him:

"Sally. Goodness, I never thought it would be you."

"Me, too, but what a pleasant and lovely surprise. I was worried about who my unknown partner might be."

Lawson took out the Cunard plastic wallet, and examined the passenger tickets:

"Ms Sally Chambers, your documents I believe." He handed them to Sally.

They had a brief hug and then quickly made their way to the departure gates and onto the magnificent Queen Mary 2. They were allocated a port-side cabin, midships on Deck Ten. The ship has a total of eighteen decks, fourteen of which are accommodation cabins. Julian and Sally entered their cabin, locked the door and each slumped into a cosy chair. They looked at each other and laughed. No words were spoken.

Julian sat quietly looking at Sally and, in his thoughts, recalled how they had first met. It was during the early days of his induction course with MI5. At home one weekend, he had been driving his Land Rover Defender truck down a country lane when he came across a broken-down Series Three Land Rover. He stopped to give assistance.

The young lady driver gave her name as Lucy and said she was waiting for her uncle to arrive to help. Julian offered to take her to a nearby pub for lunch which she accepted. He thought she was rather charming. He then dropped her off back at her vehicle, having politely declined her invitation to be taken for a meal, at a later date, as a thank-you.

The following Monday, back on the MI5 course, a presentation had been given on the capabilities of the Surveillance Team. The Head of the team then gave a practical example. He explained how they had deployed their human resources and technical equipment to undertake surveillance on an individual. This had included the use of a drone to follow the movement of their 'target' and to take photographs, when one of the team members had engaged with the target.

The Head emphasised the exercise had been undertaken to demonstrate their capabilities to the course, and also as training for his team. Much to Julian's embarrassment and annoyance the 'break down' incident, with the Land Rover, had actually been an exercise. The lady 'Lucy' was actually Sally Chambers.

Later Sally was to apologise for hurting his feelings and, once again, as a peace-offering had invited him out for a meal. He had again declined, but they parted as friends. He had last seen her, many months ago, when she unexpectedly called at his cottage one Sunday morning. He had shown her around his woodland, and, over a campfire lunch, they had discussed the strange world of MI5.

They still did not know each other's true name or background. Sally had been aware that Julian's late wife had died from cancer some three years earlier. He had politely declined to give her name, quietly saying she was from his real world and not his current existence where he only knew colleagues by their 'made-up names.'

She was also aware that since her death he had refrained from entering a personal relationship with another girl. They had departed as good friends but without any future plans to meet. Such friendships are frowned upon in the service. Close personal relationships between MI5 personnel require a confidential written report to the Human Resources Department.

When Julian had first met Sally, when she was posing as 'Lucy' with the incident of the broken-down Land Rover, he had considered she had an engagingly seductive voice. He still had that opinion. She was slim, thirty-two years of age, with long blonde hair which was often in a pony-tail and she was always stylishly dressed. She has been a member of MI5 for just over ten years and has previously indicated she did not see herself being a 'thirty-year service girl.'

For both the last few hours had been hectic, and the turn of events unexpected. Julian had anticipated catching an RAF flight back to England and spending a quiet weekend working in his Petworth woodland.

Sally had just completed attending a two-week government sponsored leadership course in New York and had intended spending a couple of days sightseeing in the Big City before catching a commercial flight back home to England.

Now, here they were together about to embark on a major operation while crossing the Atlantic Ocean.

Sally looked around and commented: "Nice cabin."

Julian smiles and makes a light-hearted comment:

"Madam, on board ship Cunard call them staterooms."

Their stateroom has the elegance and luxury of a five-star hotel. The lounge area contains a table with chairs, a separate desk with chair, a two-seater settee and two separate beds which causes Julian to comment:

"No doubt, London HQ sorted that."

The stateroom includes an open balcony overlooking the ocean.

Julian and Sally will be sharing the en-suite shower facilities. His and Her courtesy bathrobes hang on the door hooks. For the next week Julian and Sally will be working closely together on this serious and complex operation. They are two experienced professional operators, fully aware of their respective roles and responsibilities. It is a partnership of equals. They had both previously operated in situations with male and female colleagues sharing the same dangers and facilities. It will be an intense week, concentrating on the task at hand without personal distractions. Both know the rules, and there is no need for discussion.

The two agree on their cover story. Keep it brief and uncomplicated: They've been in a relationship for the past six months and have spent the previous two weeks visiting friends in Washington. Sally is a schoolteacher and Julian a self-employed business consultant. Julian explains to Sally he has been on two previous Cunard cruises with his late wife. They had sailed on the Queen Victoria, one cruise to the Mediterranean and the other to the Norwegian fjords.

The Queen Victoria is similar in design and layout to Queen Mary 2 so this should bring some benefits when navigating their way around the massive ship, which is the size of a small city. Plus, his previous experience of general life on board ship could prove useful.

The tannoy system came into life announcing all passengers were required to attend 'muster drill' and instructions were given where to assemble. Attendance is a legal requirement. Before the ship leaves harbour, muster drill must be given to prepare passengers for safe evacuation in the event of an on-board emergency. As directed, Julian and Sally collected two Life-vests from their stateroom wardrobe and made their way to the assembly point.

Back in their stateroom, and as the ship was heading towards the open sea, the next tannoy announcement was made. Passengers were invited to the Sail-away party on the open deck, with live music, to meet the captain for cocktails. Julian shook his head:

"Suggest we remain here and get on with the business."

Sally nods in agreement.

They then spent the next few hours formulating their thoughts, identifying priorities and ensuring in their minds the structures now in place, and what additional issues needed to be addressed:

- The main Command and Control Centre for Operation Dragonfly had been established at FBI Head Quarters, Washington DC. FBI World operations were controlled from this location. The senior strategy team was in place. A specific communication and research team had been activated for this operation.
- A Command Centre, with research facilities, had also been established at MI5 HQ London. It had

direct encrypted communication with FBI HQ Washington and, where required, would undertake research into passengers holding British passports.

- Within the ship a separate encrypted military satellite communication system had been installed and was active. It crewed by FBI personnel. It was for direct communications with FBI HQ. A senior FBI agent was present to direct agreed strategy.

- A separate system had been setup to actively monitor all communications being transmitted from and to the ship. This would include all passenger communication by telephone and email traffic, which by technical necessity, was registered with, and routed, via the ship's communication system.

- The ship's extensive system of CCTV operating twenty-four hours per day would l be monitored by FBI personnel.

- A SWAT team (Special Weapons And Tactics) had been deployed on the ship. They were trained to be deployed against threats of terrorism or hostage taking. The team was now located in a secure crew cabin, but away from the normal staff quarters. Their cover story was that the team of outside contractors were on board to undertake specific maintenance and electrical work. They would be wearing workmen style boiler suits which would enable them to conceal their bullet proof vests, handguns and tasers. Each would carry canvas tool-bags which would contain specialist firearms, stun guns, motion detectors and other military-style hardware. Each would be wearing a communications earpiece. With a crew of about thirteen-hundred the presence of this additional maintenance team would not arouse suspicion.

- A research team of six FBI personnel had been established and was located in a secure office facility. Their cover story was that they were undertaking a routine audit. Again, this would be regarded as a normal part of the ship's activity. The team would undertake a check of all passenger passports which, at the Check-in-Desk, had been electronically scanned with a copy of each retained. The team had secure communications with FBI HQ for World-wide record checks.

- A secure encrypted laptop had been installed in the Stateroom of Julian and Sally. The majority of their contact with FBI HQ and the relevant teams set up around the ship would be via secure Zoom-style video conferencing. When not in their stateroom the laptop computer was to be kept in the stateroom's wall safe. Their role was to liaise with senior members of the ship's management. Plus, should a British couple be identified as the likely 'assassins' Julian and Sally would endeavour to sit at their table and engage in conversation to elicit any useful information about them.

- Contingency plans were being drawn up, in conjunction with the captain and his senior team, to respond to any firearm emergency. This would include the ship's medical facilities and the secure detention room in the event of a suspect being detained.

- The ship's tannoy system could be heard throughout the vessel. Members deployed on Operation Dragonfly had been advised on the alert messages. "Maintenance engineer Johnson, code one please," would indicate that the killers had been identified and were actively preparing to undertake the killing. Personal contingency plans they had received earlier would be activated. The SWAT team would have received more detailed information and would be moving in to eliminate the threat.

- Julian and Sally's iPhones had been programmed and encrypted so as to work on board ship. In the case of an emergency, or if immediate contact with the captain was required, this method of communication would be used.

- The safety of the ship with its four-thousand passengers and crew was paramount and would remain the responsibility of the captain. Julian Lawson would ensure the captain was kept briefed on all relevant matters.

- Days three to five were consider the critical period when the attack could take place. However, the team would have to be prepared for all eventualities occurring at any time.

- Both the American and British military were aware of the potential for an incident on board QM2 and were on provisional alert. Further guidance would be forthcoming if assistance was likely to be required.

Later that evening, and having made telephone contact with the Ship's Captain, Julian and Sally visited the ship's Bridge to introduce themselves to the Staff Captain. The Bridge is located on Deck Twelve, at the foremost part of the ship and spans the entire superstructure. The Staff Captain is responsible not only for navigation, but also security and safety, and maintenance of the ship. They updated him on the current position and agree on maintaining frequent contact.

They agree that until Operation Dragonfly had been concluded, and the 'stand down' given, alcohol would not be consumed. However, with his previous knowledge of Cunard's ships, and the help of a handy pocket map, Julian gave Sally a walking tour of the ship. Back in their stateroom, they logged on to their secure laptop computer and satisfied themselves that all was quiet with no further information forthcoming.

Queen Mary 2 had departed on time at 17:00 hours from New York Brooklyn Cruise Terminal. The distance to the Port of Southampton is approximately three and a half thousand miles. The ship's average speed is twenty-four knots per hour. A nautical mile is equivalent to one point fifteen miles per hour. The ship was scheduled to berth at Southampton in the early morning of the eighth day. QM2 is an ocean liner as opposed to a cruise ship, which means she is built stronger and intended for the regular all year-round Atlantic crossing from New York to Southampton. Cruise ships do not sail the Atlantic Ocean during the worst weather months of Winter.

By 06:00 hours on the first morning on board, Julian and Sally were up and ready for business. Julian could not resist unlocking the glass sliding door and spending a relaxing ten minutes sitting in a chair on the balcony. It was a clear calm morning. The fresh smell of the sea was bracing. Sally stepped onto the balcony holding two mugs of coffee and placed one on the table next to Julian and sat down. They exchanged smiles but did not speak.

Julian and Sally then checked their laptop computer, but nothing further had been reported. So, they took the opportunity to visit the Kings Court Buffet located on Deck Seven. It is a self-service restaurant open twenty-four hours a day.

On returning to their stateroom, Sally placed a Do Not Disturb notice on the outside of the door, and Julian took the laptop computer from the wall safe. There was a message to say new intelligence was available. They logged on and engaged in a video conference with the other members of Operation Dragonfly. This included FBI HQ Washington, MI5 London and the other teams located around the ship.

Firstly, FBI Washington reported on the latest intelligence which had been obtained from the sensitive source. Apart from a few members at FBI HQ, it was not disclosed whether the 'sensitive source' was coming from a human, or technical, or an element of both. However, it was considered reliable, and with the short timescale available, the decision is that too much speculation and deviation could limit success. In simple terms: accept the available intelligence as correct and work on that basis.

So, what was the new and known intelligence:

- The assassination team consisted of a couple posing as man and wife. Their identity was still not known. They were travelling on British passports. They were considered to be extremely professional at what they do. They clearly would not travel on genuine British passports using their real names.
- Their handgun, fitted with a silencer, was already secreted on the ship when they boarded. They had no other associates or assistance on board the ship. During the cruise, to ensure secrecy, they would not have any communications with outside sources i.e.: no telephone, texting or email contact.
- The order was that the killing must be discreet with the body dumped over the side and into the sea, so that the authorities regard the disappearance as suicide or that the man fell overboard late at night whilst drunk.
- No further information was currently available regarding the possible identity of the killer's intended victim. The source was adamant he was a resident in the UK but cannot confirm he was actually British or that he was a British passport holder.

From the intelligence then available, the analysts had identified many questions:

1. The killers possessed British passports, but were they British?
2. Were their passports forgeries or had they falsely obtained genuine British passports?

3. What was the reason for wanting to kill the unknown victim?

4. Why was the killing planned to take place on the New York to Southampton route?

5. Why go to the trouble, danger and expense of undertaking the killing on a cruise ship? Possibly, to ensure that with the body dumped fifteen hundred miles out at sea there would be no evidence to indicate a crime had been committed.

6. On the evidence at present available, the killers were possibly British, and the victim lived in Britain. So, how did both parties get to America?

7. If the victim travelled from Southampton to America by ship, why did the plan to kill him not take place then?

8. Could this indicate the victim did not travel to America by ship?

9. How and when did he arrive in America?

10. Likewise, how and when did the killers arrive in America.

For the first phase of the operation, priority would be given to checking the British passports to identify if any are forgeries. The assumption being made, in this first round of analysis, was that the killers were fit and in the younger age group of passengers. Therefore, priority would be given to checking the details of passengers fifty years or younger. It was considered unlikely that the killers, would have travelled before using their current identities. So, included in the priority search they would look for current passengers who had no prior history of travelling with the Cunard Line.

Julian sought clarification about the terminology being used to describe the couple they were endeavouring to identify. Reports coming from the sensitive source used the term 'assassins.' Julian asked if this is the term actually being used. In its correct usage, an assassin is a professional killer of a politically prominent person.

It was confirmed; the intelligence reports used the term assassins, but equally they had been described as professional killers. There was nothing to suggest the intended victim was a political figure. The analysts said most identified assassins had served in the military, in a special services unit, and were in the thirty to forty years of age group.

Day Two at Sea. It was another early start to the day. Julian began by enjoying a relaxing fifteen minutes sitting on the balcony quietly contemplating what the day had in store. Sally joined him bringing with her two mugs of coffee and placed them on the small table. She remained standing and rested her hands on the balcony rail looking out to sea.

After a minute of silence, Sally turned to face Julian and smiled:

"This is all so unreal. Yet, at the same time, so special."

He smiled and nodded in agreement.

They then visited the Kings Court Buffet on Deck Seven for a Continental breakfast.

At 08:00 hours they were back in their stateroom to begin the first video conference call of the day with FBI HQ Washington, MI5 HQ London and the teams located on board QM2. The representatives from FBI HQ reported that they were making good progress although, at present, there were no positive results to identify the potential killers.

They had prioritised the search parameters to optimise the available resources to achieve the best chance of success. Restricting the areas for research brings with it the dangers of missing potentially vital information but, in view of the short timescale, it was a calculated risk that must be taken.

In the first phase, all British passports had been electronically scanned with the details checked against USA and UK data bases. Anomalies and inconsistency were found with some, but not considered relevant to the current investigation. The suggested profile for a professional killer is between the ages of twenty-four to forty years. The decision had been taken, for the present, to eliminate from further research, British passport holders aged fifty years and older.

Having significantly reduced the volume of passports, the second phase is now underway with more detailed research being undertaken into the personal background of each passport holder. In respect of each, their tickets for the cruise were being researched to establish when, where and by whom they were purchased. Plus, the date and method of purchase.

The team monitoring all communication emanating from and to the ship gave an update on its findings.

All passengers on Cunard voyages receive complimentary Internet time. The hours allocated are dependent on various factors but vary from two to ten hours per voyage. The team noted that the majority of passengers take up the offer to use the facility in their staterooms.

The team suggested their analysis of the passengers' email content had given them an indication of who were not the killers, rather than identify the likely killers. The team had noted, intelligence from the 'sensitive source' had previously said that the killers, whilst on board ship, would not communicate with their 'sponsor.' No information in the communications traffic had identified any suspicious activity to suggest contact.

Examples of email content included: selfie photographs and of meals to impress family and friends about their luxury cruise. Then there was the husband cheating on his wife and secretly contacting his mistress. There was even one email entirely typed in code, which the analysts quickly unscrambled. It revealed the sender was giving instructions about a tax avoidance scheme he was involved with. Not the behaviour one would expect killers to undertake. For the present, this group of people would not be the subject of further checks.

The team posed the question: in this computer savvy age, and with free Internet access available, why would a fee-paying passenger not take up the offer to use the Internet for business or family contact? The team suggested non take up of the offer might indicate the relevant passengers were being ultra-security conscious about their presence on board ship. A list of passengers who had not taken up the offer had been drawn up and was being submitted for further research.

At 16:00 hours, Julian and Sally were sampling the delights of the ship's traditional afternoon tea and cakes in the large, elegant Queens Room on Deck Three. This is the indulgent hour held each and every day. It is Cunard's prized daily ritual for passengers to gather in comfort to sit and consume scones and pastries with cups of fresh tea. Julian received a text message for them to return to their stateroom and login to an urgent video conference call. There had been a significant breakthrough.

Back in their stateroom, with the door locked, and a Do Not Disturb notice in place, Julian logged on for a video conference with the other participants. Sally sat next to him, so both were visible on screen for the conference. The latest information was very encouraging. The research teams in Washington, London and on the ship had been in constant communication, working around the clock, and were optimistic that the two suspects had now been identified.

The various research looking at British passport holders, the background of their Cunard tickets and the list of passengers who had not taken up the offer of free Internet use, identified an interesting match for a couple with an address in Surrey in southern England. The passports were in the names James and Diana Church.

The MI5 London team came into view. It was Director Jane Rigby.

"Good day Julian and Sally. Several hours ago, Special Branch officers visited the house of Mr and

Mrs Church in Godalming, Surrey and found them at home. We have checked them out and can confirm the genuine James and Diana Church are safely at home."

Jane consulted her notes and continued:

"They have never been on a cruise. Three months ago, their house in Godalming was broken into when they were on a day trip to London. The burglary was reported to the local police and remains undetected. Some valuable and sentimental jewellery was stolen. Until Special Branch visited today, the couple had not realised their passports had been stolen. Apart from informing them their details have been used by a couple on a Cunard cruise, they are not aware of this operation. However, they have been told they must not disclose the Special Branch visit to anyone."

The conference welcomed the encouraging news and discussion continues. New information was being received as the conference progressed. The latest information had identified that the Mr and Mrs Church, on board ship, only arrived in New York two days prior to the departure of QM2. They had flown in on a scheduled flight from Johannesburg International Airport, South Africa, using the British issued passports.

This latest evidence had now confirmed the presence, on board ship, of a couple using false identities with stolen British passports containing replaced photographs. The intelligence suggested their intention was to kill, but evidence was still required to prove the case. There was much work still to do, and little time left to ensure the killing did not take place. The identity of the intended victim remains unknown.

The conference discussed the actions that needed to be put in place without delay. The research and monitoring teams would continue with their work. The FBI couple, who were on ship posing as passengers, would discreetly undertake surveillance on the couple Mr and Mrs Church and report back on their movements. It might well be that they were keeping a watch on the movement of their intended victim. This might well be the way the team would be able to identify him.

The SWAT team had been briefed and were on standby, with no deployment required at this stage. The ship's captain had received confidential notice that the couple had been identified.

The first black-tie dinner of the cruise would be that evening. The ship had several restaurants, the main dining room being the Britannia Restaurant with a capacity to seat one thousand diners. Mr and Mrs Church were scheduled for the first sitting at 18:30 hours. The evening Gala Ball commenced at 20:00 hours in the Queens Room. Throughout the ship there were many evening activities to satisfy every need of the almost three thousand passengers, including the Royal Court Theatre to the large Empire Casino and the Mayfair Shopping deck.

During the evening, if circumstances allowed, Julian and Sally would endeavour to get into conversation with the two suspects, as fellow British passengers, and hopefully gain useful intelligence on them. For the evening's activities Julian would hire a dinner jacket from the Mayfair clothing store.

The couple, Mr and Mrs Church, occupied a stateroom on Deck Eight. It was located on the Port side of the ship and had a balcony. When seated for the beginning of their evening meal, members of the SWAT team would undertake covert entry into their stateroom to obtain fingerprint impressions and DNA samples. Covert equipment would also be installed to actively monitor the couple.

During the late afternoon, the two suspects were observed together leaving their stateroom. They then split up and spent an hour separately walking slowly around the ship visiting different decks and various open spaces, from the shopping area to the cocktail bars and restaurants. The FBI couple, after undertaking surveillance, reported back that they appeared to be searching for someone, but without success.

Covert photographs of the suspects were obtained. The man was described as slim with an athletic physique and about thirty-five years of age. He fitted the suggested profile for a professional killer. The FBI couple were directed to continue with the surveillance and alert Control when the suspects, Mr and Mrs Church, were seated in the Britannia Restaurant for their evening meal.

Julian and Sally arrived back at their stateroom, Julian with his hired dinner jacket and Sally with a ball gown she has also hired. They were expected to blend in with the evening events and, hopefully, engage with the two suspects, so wearing the correct attire was essential.

They logged on to their computer for a brief video conference update. Colour photographs of the two suspects were now available to view. It was agreed that Julian and Sally would dress in their newly acquired evening wear and attend the Britannia Restaurant for the 18:30 hours sitting.

Prior to attending the restaurant, from the team monitoring the ship's extensive CCTV system, Julian and Sally were given details of where the two suspects, Mr and Mrs Church, were dining. The suspects had chosen to occupy a table-for-two located at the far end of the restaurant, no doubt, as a deliberate ploy to avoid sharing a table, and conversation, with other passengers. Similarly, Julian and Sally secured a table-for-two some distance away, but with the suspects in view.

Julian and Sally enjoyed a full four-course meal but declined the offer of wine. They engaged in small-talk about their walk around the ship and its amenities, deliberately avoiding any reference to Operation Dragonfly.

As they left the restaurant, Julian quietly commented:

"Sally, may I say you look gorgeous."

In a playful mood she gently punched him on the shoulder: "Thank you partner."

They strolled slowly to a nearby cocktail bar and ordered coffees. The open double-doors to the restaurant remained in their view. They were waiting for the two suspects to leave. In this massive ship, which of the many evening activities would Mr and Mrs Church choose to attend?

Julian and Sally did not have to wait long. The two suspects left the restaurant and walked in the direction of the Queens Room, which is where the evening Gala Ball was being held.

Julian leaned across the coffee table and whispered:

"Notice anything odd in their manner?"

"Yes. From leaving their table, walking across the length of the restaurant and on towards the Queens Room, there has been no speaking or contact. Just like a couple of strangers."

Julian replied: "It could be the pressure of what's on their minds."

They got up to follow the two suspects, at a discreet distance. Julian took Sally by the hand and whispered:

"We can't have our cover blown, we'd better act like a loving couple."

They walked towards the Queens Room, hand in hand. Sally did not object.

For the Gala Ball the large Queens Room had been configured, with a dance floor in the centre, and tables and chairs arranged around the sides. As with their dining arrangements, the suspects again chose to sit at a table-for-two. Julian and Sally sat nearby, but the likelihood of developing any conversation with them seemed out of the question.

Mr and Mrs Church departed after about twenty minutes and entered the nearby central lift. Julian watched the digital floor indicator above the closing door. The lift stopped at Deck Eight. He felt satisfied that the team monitoring the CCTV would have them in their sights and watch them enter their stateroom.

Julian and Sally returned to their stateroom and logged-on for a video conference update: The two suspects, Mr and Mrs Church, were now safely back in their stateroom on Deck Eight. They appeared to be preparing to bed-down for the night. Their activities in the stateroom were being monitored covertly. The corridor of Deck Eight was being monitored constantly. Two members of the SWAT team had taken up residence in a vacant stateroom at the end of Deck Eight.

The identity of the intended victim was still unknown. If during the night there was any indication that the suspects might be preparing to leave their stateroom additional resources, including two other members of the SWAT team, plus Julian and Sally would be deployed.

The senior strategic team at FBI HQ Washington, in conjunction with MI5 HQ London, had reviewed the position. The intelligence from the 'sensitive source' had so far proved correct. However, to reiterate, the only evidence currently available to support a criminal prosecution was that two suspects were on board ship using false identification.

The second element of the intelligence was that the suspects were on board to kill. To detain the suspects now would result in failure to satisfactorily resolve the case. To allow the operation to continue brought additional dangers. The safety of the four thousand passengers and crew was paramount. The ship's captain was consulted.

At the commencement of Operation Dragonfly, the American and British Military were advised and placed on standby. The decision was that the operation would be permitted to continue. Additional resources were to be deployed, if required, to ensure a successful outcome without compromising the safety of the ship.

Queen Mary 2 was currently just over one thousand nautical miles out of New York steaming to Portsmouth with another two thousand five hundred miles to travel. It was anticipated that the attack on the intended, but so far unidentified, victim was planned to take place in a day or so and during the hours of darkness.

The United States Second Fleet HQ, Norfolk, Virginia had been briefed. An amphibious assault ship was already in the North Atlantic making its way to an agreed position. It was a large special purpose ship with helicopters and landing craft in its armoury. It also had elite special operations personnel on board, known as Navy SEALs (Sea, Air, and Land Teams).

In the next few hours, during darkness, the assault ship would stand-off about six miles from QM2. A Navy SEALs ten-man team would be deployed in a high speed eleven-metre-long Rigid Hull inflatable boat to come along side and board QM2. The transfer of the Navy SEALs had been scheduled to take place at 02:30 hours.

A landing of the team by helicopter had been considered but rejected as the noise would attract too much attention. A sea approach, during darkness, could be achieved with the minimum of attention. Once the team were on board, they would remain until the conclusion of the operation, and the assault ship would steam out of sight of the QM2.

At 02:30 hours everything was in place for the boarding. QM2 continued on the same course but at reduced speed. The Rigid Hull inflatable, with the fully-equipped ten-man SEAL team, approached from the stern of the ship and alongside positioning the craft under the gangway. A rope ladder had been put in place by selected members of the ship's deck crew. The transfer of the team was swift and without incident. The Rigid Hull inflatable returned to the waiting assault ship.

Arrangements had been made for the team to be housed in a secure and isolated area in the lower hold of the ship. The senior officer from the FBI SWAT team joined them for a briefing.

Julian and Sally, plus the other participants in Operation Dragonfly, were immediately contacted and informed of the arrival of the Navy SEALs.

At 03:00 hours a joint video conference was held to ensure all teams were fully updated. Two Navy SEALs were deployed to Deck Eight to join the two SWAT members residing in one of the staterooms. FBI HQ Washington reported on the result on the DNA samples, which had been fast-tracked for analysis, taken covertly from the stateroom of the two suspects. Both samples indicate Eastern European ancestry: most likely from Russia or Belarus.

Day Three at Sea. It was another early start. Julian and Sally logged-on to the video conference with the normal participants. The FBI HQ Washington representative reported that the additional resources had been deployed, giving confidence that the two suspects would be the subject of a full surveillance capability should they leave their stateroom. It was viewed with concern that the identity of the intended victim was still not known.

The information from the 'sensitive source' had indicated the victim held a British passport, although the indication was that he was not born in the UK but was now resident in London. Further, the intended killers were referred to as assassins. There was speculation that the intended victim was actually a Russian oligarch who had moved to the UK many years ago. No doubt, having transferred his billions of dollars out of Russia and, thus, the reason for the proposed assassination.

Extensive research had been undertaken, and continued to be so, to review the background and financial status of the identified rich passengers travelling on the ship. To-date, none fit the profile of the unknown victim.

QM2 has some of the most expensive and luxurious accommodation of any cruise ship. The Queens Grill Suites include personal butler service and in-suite dining. The cost per person per night commences at over two thousand pounds. Many would be accompanied by their own staff and were extremely private and secretive, having no direct contact with the ship's staff.

The latest information about the two suspects, Mr and Mrs Church, gave their DNA profile of Eastern European ancestry, most likely from Russia or Belarus. This added credence to the suggestion that it is a Russian assassination team hunting down a Russian billionaire oligarch, a fairly common occurrence since the collapse of the Soviet Union. Previous intelligence had identified the two had flown into New York from South Africa. Enquires had not found any evidence to indicate they were ever in the UK.

The two suspects had breakfast served in their stateroom on Deck Eight. Close monitoring on them continued, with two teams on standby to be deployed should they leave their room.

At midday, the female left the room on her own. A surveillance team followed her. The man remained in the room and sat in an armchair placing a brown leather shoulder bag on his lap. After a while he flipped open the bag and took out a handgun fitted with a silencer. His actions were recorded on the covert camera system. It is the first time the monitoring team had seen him with a gun.

The information was immediately conveyed to Central Control and relayed to the relevant teams. This added some additional urgency and danger to the operation. The preparedness level was upgraded. Four members of the Navy SEALs team were issued with civilian casual clothes and deployed as backup to the SWAT surveillance teams. The ship's captain was briefed.

Surveillance on the female suspect, Mrs Church, continued as she walked around the ship visiting various amenities on different decks. She did not appear to be looking for anyone. Eventually, she stopped at one of the smaller restaurants and ordered lunch. She did not appear in any rush to return to her stateroom.

It was 15:30 hours. The male suspect, Mr Church, remained in his stateroom, on his own, just resting in the armchair with his eyes closed. There was no sign of his female partner returning. Had they already identified their intended victim and were just waiting for the right time to strike?

The sensitive source intelligence had reported that the killing would take place during the hours of darkness, possibly in the early morning before daybreak. Central Control were now considering if it might occur earlier and at some quiet location on the ship.

16:00 hours. The male suspect, Mr Church, checked his wristwatch and slowly got to his feet. He left the stateroom with the brown leather bag over his left shoulder. It contained the gun fitted with a silencer.

The various Operation Dragonfly teams were alerted to this latest development. He took the lift to Deck Three and walked to the Chart Room. This was a public area for the passengers to view the ship's navigation charts and check on the progress of the cruise. He stopped and consulted the main chart on which was plotted the ship's progress, the distance travelled and current position.

He then walked towards the middle section of the ship and descended the central stairs to Deck Two. He loitered for a moment, quickly looking around the concourse, then briskly entered the lavishly furnished Empire Casino, with its gaming tables and numerous slot machines. He strolled around, stopping occasionally, to take an interest in the card games being played. He did not participate. After fifteen minutes he walked out of the casino and took a seat at a coffee lounge nearby. Again, he appeared to be monitoring his surroundings.

He ordered a coffee, appearing relaxed but with a constant gaze on the people playing in the casino. His attention appeared to be fixed on one particular man. A short stocky man, about sixty years of age. The surveillance team were watching from a discreet distance.

After thirty minutes the short stocky man left the casino and ascended the nearby central stairs to Deck

Three and walked towards the shopping area. He was followed at a distance by 'Mr Church' still carrying his brown leather shoulder bag, which he was gripping with his left hand. The surveillance team, operating in separate pairs, were not far behind. This movement of 'Mr Church' was clear confirmation that the intended killer had identified his target. The game was on.

The intended victim, the short stocky man, entered one of the shops and made a purchase of a packet of sweets. He then descended back down the stairs and re-entered the Empire Casino, followed by 'Mr Church.' One pair of the surveillance team followed. A member of the other team immediately walked into the shop. With a quick glance at the digital display on the electronic till he was able to note the stateroom number of the last customer. No cash is used on board ship. All purchases are made using a passenger's security and door entry swipe card.

The short stocky man took up his previous position at the gaming table, with 'Mr Church' taking up his previous seat at the coffee bar. The surveillance team are now also back in position.

Details of the stateroom number are immediately passed to Central Control. Within fifteen minutes an urgent message was relayed back to the surveillance team:

'Please confirm the deck and stateroom number is correct.' Confirmation was given.

Central Control was dubious. The number given was for a small inside stateroom: being in the cheapest cost category for the ship's accommodation. Central Control asked for further clarification.

Discreetly, one of the surveillance team entered the casino and acted as an interested observer of the game being played. He ensured he was near to the 'victim' who was using his passenger security and door swipe card to purchase the required gaming chips.

The team member reported back to Central Control:

'Room number, as previously given, is correct.'

This presented a conundrum. The intelligence said the intended target was a Russian billionaire oligarch. The man in the casino would appear to be of very modest means. MI5 HQ London had undertaken research into the man and, the initial report back confirmed he was indeed a man of modest means. It would appear the killer has identified the wrong man. No doubt, suggested Central Control, the mistake would become obvious when the man was followed back to his small, inside stateroom.

Still sitting at the coffee bar, 'Mr Church' was becoming uneasy. He appeared to be troubled and concerned. He stood up and walked away from the coffee bar area. He ascended the stairs to Deck Three, And slowly walked along the row of shops, stopping briefly to look at a window display. He then moved on before, again, stopping. He was not actually viewing the display but rather checking on the reflections from the glass. He walked, suddenly stopped, turned and walked back in the opposite direction. He was employing tradecraft: Anti-surveillance techniques.

He descended the stairs and sat back at the coffee bar and ordered another coffee and leaned back in the chair trying to appear casual. In fact, he was very alert to what was going on around him.

It was now late afternoon with many passengers walking through the main concourse and into the various public bars and restaurants. To his left, some distance away, he noted two men sitting together. Both in their late twenties, slim and fit looking, with noticeably short hair. Not the typical profile for passengers on a cruise ship. Then, to his right he observed two men casually walking around the concourse, similar in age and physique to the other two men.

He stood up and quickly walked to the nearby Gents toilet. He walked through the open entrance; walked past the long row of cubicles and out the exit without stopping. The man had clearly given up keeping observation on his target who was still at the gaming table in the casino. He was now certain he was under surveillance by a team of at least four, and probably many more. This was serious. Survival was his priority.

He headed to the central staircase, gripping his brown leather bag with his left hand. The bag contained his gun. It would be loaded and ready for action. If immediate danger presented itself, he would pull the flap open with his left hand and in a single motion have the gun firmly in his right hand ready for action.

From Deck Three, he walked quickly to the starboard side of the ship and into the accommodation corridor. He ascended the stairs in the accommodation area of the ship, deck after deck, until he reached Deck Eight. He was now almost at running pace. His progress was being monitored on CCTV. The contingency plan was now being deployed.

Most of the FBI staff, who were fully trained agents and who had for the past few days been involved in research functions, were now out of their offices assisting to close down potential escape routes and ensure the safety of passengers and crew. All FBI staff undertaking this active role were armed with handguns, and with earpieces, in constant communication with Central Control.

As he ran along the corridor and approached his stateroom, he took out his gun with the muzzle pointing upwards. By his actions, his military training was obvious. He moved cautiously but deliberately sweeping his gun from side to side. He was ready and prepared to confront and deal with anyone who might attempt to block his progress.

Central Control sent out an alert warning to Operation Dragonfly personnel:

'Target is armed and ready.'

The door to his stateroom was already open, with a laundry trolley stationed nearby. A young chambermaid walked out carrying her cleaning equipment. She was startled by seeing a man running towards her with a gun. She stopped, screamed and dropped her equipment. He grabbed her roughly by her neck and pulled her into the stateroom. He then kicked the door closed and pushed her onto the bed. She was terrified.

Central Control sent out a further warning:

'Target has one hostage. Situation is contained.'

Lockdown of this section on Deck Eight was complete. The area was secured. Nearby staterooms had been evacuated. Security screens had been erected. With cruise ships, and their passengers often elderly, death on board is not an uncommon occurrence. Passengers who frequently travel on cruise ships will have experienced staterooms and adjoining areas being screened off following a sudden death. Passengers would not be aware, or told, of the true nature of what is happening. Bad news is never broadcast on a holiday cruise ship!

Central Control was monitoring what was happening in this stateroom. The Young Filipino chambermaid remained lying on the bed. She had been instructed not to move and would obey his every word. He sat in the armchair holding the gun and pointing it towards the locked door. He was a trained professional and knows the likely outcome. He sat quietly contemplating his fate. There was no escape.

The ship was fifteen-hundred miles out at sea from land. He had a hostage, but his options were limited. If he attempted to leave the room with her, where would they go. He was on his own, with no backup or assistance, and with the prospect of another three plus days at sea. There was evidently a full military team on board. If captured, he faced the prospect of a life in prison.

He unlocked the sliding door to the balcony and walked out clutching the rail with his left hand and continuing to hold the gun in his right hand. He leaned over the rail, quickly checking to his left and then to his right. In the darkness, he then looked up, and down to the sea below. There is no sign of activity. His thought process is that a military assault might come via the balcony. For him to contemplate escaping via the balcony was futile.

The telephone on the desk rang. He didn't answer it. It continued to ring, but he made no effort to answer it. He was a highly trained soldier with a Special Forces background. On the other end of the telephone would be a trained negotiator, sitting with other psychological experts, reading a carefully crafted script to convince him it was in his best interest to surrender. No, he would not play their game. He came to complete a killing mission. It had been aborted. Surrender or suicide were not options he would consider. He knew it would end with his death.

The senior team in Central Control wished the situation to be resolved safely and successfully without delay. This was also the requirement of the ship's captain. Should they wait a little longer? Could they get a message to him, via some other means, that if he did not surrender an armed assault of the room would be undertaken? That was considered a dangerous option. His likely response would be to physically take hold of the chambermaid and threaten to kill her if an assault on the room was attempted. Currently, covert CCTV inside the room showed she was safely lying on the bed.

The subject would not be permitted to leave the stateroom with his hostage and, by refusing to communicate on the telephone, it was evident he was not prepared to enter into negotiation. With the SWAT and Navy SEALs teams on board, Central Control had all the human and technical weaponry to bring the matter to a swift conclusion. The authorisation was given to proceed. Command was officially transferred to the senior officer commanding the Navy SEALs. The motto of the Navy SEALs is: 'The only easy day was yesterday.'

The door to the stateroom was locked. However, the electronic locking mechanism could be overridden from the ship's control centre. The subject was armed and clearly intent to use his firearm if an entry was attempted. His gun was pointed towards the door. The hostage was lying on the bed, to the left of the door. She was not in the line of fire of the subject, nor of military personnel entering the room.

Two Navy SEALs were quietly positioned, in the crouching position, either side of the locked door with their rifles in the ready to fire stance. They were wearing body armour vests with full combat clothing with balaclavas. They were equipped with M4A1 carbine automatic rifles fitted with silencers and laser aiming sights.

Two other members of the team, similarly equipped, stood either side of the door, with rifles in the ready to attack position. These two would be the first to open fire when the door was opened. On a given command, from the ship's control centre, the door would automatically unlock and the ceiling lighting in the room and in the corridor would be switched off leaving the area in darkness.

All personnel confirmed they were in position and ready to proceed. The command was given to STRIKE. The area was in instant darkness. The sound of a click was heard as the electronic door-lock was deactivated. The kneeling soldier to the left, punched the door wide open. The two standing soldiers each took one side-step to the centre of the open doorway and, with rifles pointing towards the dark shadow, together released a burst of rapid fire. There was minimum noise from the gunfire then silence.

Lights were then switched back on. The subject was incapacitated, laying on the floor. The chambermaid was swiftly taken away to safety. She was unharmed. As was the policy in such matters, the Navy SEALs retreated back to their holding bay in the lower section of the ship. They would have their own separate debrief. Their identities would not be known to the other security agencies.

After the Navy SEALs departed, Julian was the first to enter the stateroom. He knelt by the gravely wounded man. There was no sense of drama. The man was barely conscious. Blood was oozing from his mouth. He looked at Julian as if he wanted to speak.

Julian moved his head closer. The man whispered:

"One of yours, I believe."

Julian simply said: "Pardon" as if seeking an explanation.

The man's head flopped back. He was dead. Other members of the team were now present in the room.

Without ceremony, the dead man was placed into a plastic body-bag and taken away. The room was searched, and various items removed. The stateroom was then sealed. Repairs would be undertaken to mend the bullet holes in the walls.

Within an hour the screens in the corridor were removed. As far as the passengers were concerned it was just another death onboard. Life and the cruise would continue as normal.

Julian and Sally returned to their stateroom, and log-on to their computer for a team video conference with all relevant participants. Operation Dragonfly was deemed a success. The assassin was dead. The threat had been eliminated and the victim was safe. The female member of the team had been detained and, in due course as she had no known connection to the UK, would be taken back to America with the FBI for interview. She was currently refusing to speak.

The body of the man would also be taken back to America, with the FBI undertaking investigation into his background and his likely Russian connections.

The consensus expressed by the senior command team was that the intended 'killers' had evidently misidentified their intended victim. The man they thought they had identified as their victim was in fact a British subject of modest means.

The real target still had not been identified. He was, no doubt, one of the people residing in one of the luxury suites who did not mix with the normal passengers with their privacy closely protected by their own staff. They would not take kindly to being interviewed by FBI and MI5 officers. Neither would the cruise company wish for their most valuable customers to be annoyed by such intrusion. Far better not to take the matter further.

The man who had been mistaken for the assassin's target would not be told of the events. It would cause him unnecessary concern and spoil his holiday.

Within the hour, the Navy SEALs had departed QM2 and were on their way back to their own support ship.

Julian and Sally visited QM2's Bridge to give the Ship's Captain and the Staff Captain a final debrief and to thank them for their assistance.

As far as Julian and Sally were concerned, the MI5 involvement in Operation Dragonfly was concluded. They had one last video conference call with Director Jane Rigby to ensure all areas had been covered. In due course, they would prepare a classified report on the operation. Jane thanked the pair for their efforts and told them to enjoy the rest of the cruise relaxing.

They ended the day with a late evening visit to the Kings Court Buffet. Tomorrow they would relax and enjoy the facilities.

Day Four at Sea. Julian was now into his daily routine of a 06:00 hours sit on the balcony for fifteen minutes of quiet contemplation. Sally joined him with two mugs of coffee. They briefly mentioned the previous day's events. Witnessing death was never a pleasant experience. They agreed not to discuss the issue for the next couple of days and try to relax.

Sally was keen to see the amenities on the ship and enjoy some of the activities. A visit to one of the five swimming pools and to the gymnasium was on her agenda. Julian was a keen photographer. He intended to spend part of the day strolling around the twelve decks, publicly accessible to passengers, indulging in his hobby.

After an enjoyable relaxing day, the pair visited the Britannia Restaurant for the 18:30 hours sitting. They shared a table with two other couples and chose the a la carte five-course menu. The meal was excellent, and they enjoyed the relaxed conversation with the other people sharing the table.

Julian then suggested they visit the Commodore Club, forward of the ship on Deck Nine. It had a luxurious and relaxed atmosphere where live music was played. Each of the three Cunard ships has a Commodore Club. Julian said he enjoyed visiting the club when he sailed on the Queen Victoria. They had their first alcoholic drink since joining the ship. With Operation Dragonfly concluded alcohol was back on the menu! A large single malt whisky for Julian and cocktails for Sally.

They were back in their stateroom by 23:00 hours. The chambermaid had turned back the bedcovers and placed the traditional chocolate on each pillow. They agreed it had been an enjoyable evening. Each sat in the comfy armchairs and spoke about the genuine and pleasant people they had met over dinner. Julian was back in reflective mood.

"That was one of the most relaxing and enjoyable evenings I've had for a long time. I still feel unhappy living a lie."

"Living a lie?" responded Sally."

"They were lovely, friendly people telling us about their lives and families. Then in answer to their questions I told them about us. All lies, fiction, a total false narrative. I don't like myself for doing it."

"Just think of it as acting. We're just playing a part."

"I don't want to get too deep but," he hesitated and then continued: "I looked across at you when you were telling them about our lives together. It sounded good, but none of it true."

"So, what is beneath what you are trying to say?" asked Sally.

He gave a smile: "You sounded so genuine telling your untruths. In a strange way that hurts me."

Sally smiled and frowned but didn't speak.

Julian looked slightly embarrassed:

"I respect you. Care for you and, perhaps more, much more."

Sally replied:

"Thank you. Perhaps, there could be a different life around the corner."

Two further relaxing and enjoyable days followed. They took advantage of the facilities and enjoyed the excellent meals in the different restaurants.

On day six at sea, with clear skies, Julian was up early before dawn with his camera on the top open deck to photograph the spectacular sunrise: to capture that instant when the Sun appeared in the east on the horizon. The QM2 is one of the World's largest movable structures with a displacement weight of over seventy-nine thousand tonnes and a length of three-hundred-and-forty-five metres.

Standing on the forward observation deck he marvelled at this mammoth metal structure slicing effortlessly through the Atlantic Ocean at twenty-five knots per hour. It is so large and powerful, yet at this instant it feels so small.

He stands alone with his thoughts. Most of the four thousand people aboard the vessel will still be asleep in their beds. The ship was over two-thousand miles from the nearest land. At this point the depth of the ocean was over five-thousand metres. He was so high up on the ship that when he looked to the horizon, he could see the curvature of the Earth. Yet, in all that vast ocean and distance there was not one other vessel in view. A truly magical time of day and a special place to be.

Following the conclusion of Operation Dragonfly, Julian was determined to have a restful few days and not think about his work. However, one issue kept reoccurring in his mind. A nagging feeling that something wasn't quite right. It was to do with the last words spoken by the dying 'Mr Church.' He had whispered with his last breath:

'One of yours, I believe.'

Julian repeated the words back in his mind and pondered on the meaning. Was 'Mr Church' simply saying the soldier who shot him was on Julian's team or was there another explanation?

Julian did not include in his report the last words spoken by 'Mr Church.' Neither had he mentioned the matter to Sally or Director Jane Rigby.

CHAPTER NINE

Return to the UK

As scheduled, Queen Mary 2 berthed, during the early morning of the eighth day at sea, at the Port of Southampton, England. Julian and Sally had developed a good working relationship: and it had deliberately remained a professional and business one. Both knew they shared a fondness for each other.

It was just after 08:00 hours when they disembarked. Standing together in the Arrival Lounge with their respective luggage, they hadn't actually spoken about getting home. There was clearly some sadness, on the part of each, that they would now be parting.

Julian took the initiative:

"My cottage is about sixty miles from here. I was intending to take a taxi. Why not join me? Then we can have lunch at my place, and, in the afternoon, I'll drive you home."

Sally agreed and together they embark on a taxi journey to his cottage on the outskirts of Petworth, in the county of West Sussex. Sally had visited his cottage some months before, when they had enjoyed a happy day in his woodland.

Arriving at his cottage, they sat down with a much-needed mug of fresh coffee. Julian had promised to cook lunch but opening the fridge it was almost empty. Without much thought, he said:

"No problem. The general store is only a couple of miles away. Let's drive into town and get some provisions."

So off they drove in his Land Rover Defender truck and parked near to the general store. Julian picked up and handed a wire basket to Sally:

"Please choose the food and I'll sort out the wine and beer."

Brenda, the store manager, had seen them enter the store and had given Julian a welcoming smile.

Sally asked Brenda a question about some bread. In responding Brenda inadvertently called her 'Lucy.'

Julian, who was standing close by gently corrected her: "It's Sally."

Brenda smiles: "Sorry Ben. Clumsy me."

Sally was a little confused. 'Lucy' had been the false name she had used during the 'broken down Land Rover' exercise' when Julian was on the MI5 training course. How did Brenda know? Why had she called her Lucy?

When Julian was out of earshot, Sally quietly asked Brenda why she had called her Lucy.

Brenda was very apologetic:

"Sorry, I wasn't thinking. Ben's late wife was called Lucy."

Julian joined Sally at the store counter and paid in cash for the provisions. He was not aware of the conversation Sally had with Brenda. They drove back to his cottage and together they prepared lunch.

As Julian was setting the table, Sally mischievously called out from the kitchen: "Ben."

"Yes." He stopped and returned to the kitchen. He looked at Sally and smiled:

"Back at the general store, I realised Brenda had used my real name. Yes, I am Ben Swan."

Sally moved closer and hugged him by his arm:

"I like the name Ben. I'm sorry for using the name Lucy back on the Land Rover exercise, I honestly didn't know it was the name of your late wife."

He commented with a smile:

"A man with two names. Could get confusing. Let's have lunch and we can have a long chat afterwards."

After some light-hearted discussion, and for obvious practical reasons, they agreed the name 'Julian' should continue to be used. Perhaps, in the future, the position might change.

Following lunch they walked together along the grassy track to the log cabin, which was located in the beech-tree section of the woodland. Julian was proud of the cabin, which he built in his woodland. Sally had visited the cabin during her previous visit and was aware just how much he enjoyed the simple pleasure of being there.

Together they gathered logs and started a small campfire. He opened up the cabin and brought out two old, but comfy, chairs which he placed near the fire. They sat and talked. Sally couldn't avoid mentioning that she liked the name 'Ben.' This triggered more conversation about cover identities being essential for personnel working within British Intelligence.

Julian said he could understand the need to operate with a cover identity. It was a secret organisation. If one officer were identified, or went rogue, then the whole system wouldn't collapse like a pack of cards. He was aware that disclosure of one's true identity would hinder promotion prospects. He suggested it was not so important in his case. Under his true identity he was known as a police officer and, in the future, he would resume life in that role. He joked that he was not trying to climb the greasy pole in MI5 to reach the position of Director General.

In answer to Sally's questions, he confirmed that when he visited his Mother and family, which was rare because of current circumstances, he was 'Ben Swan, a policeman.' Sally acknowledged the same applied with her when she visited her parents. Both agreed it was a crazy secret existence.

Sally took the initiative:

"Come Monday morning, we'll be back in our respective departments within this large organisation. In the course of our work, we might bump into each other once every six months. So, what's the future?"

She was in a playful mood, but the question had a serious edge to it.

Julian responded:

"During Operation Dragonfly we worked together as a professional team and in a business manner. That was correct."

After a pause: "But secretly, especially when I saw you in that evening dress, I did think how gorgeous you looked."

Then after a further pause he added with a laugh: "I also, thought what a bloody liar you were."

Sally interrupted: "But a good one."

Julian, with a smile, added:

"No more beating around the bush. How about submitting the necessary report in triplicate to Human Resources saying we're in a relationship?"

Sally looked happy:

"Yes, please. Finally, we can act like a couple of normal adults."

Julian added:

"There's one condition. If it turns out that your true name is Gertrude or something similar the deal is off."

They had much to discuss and decide in the coming months. For the present, Julian drove Sally back to London.

Sally Chambers was thirty-two years of age. She was recruited into the service from university. She owned a modern one-bedroom apartment on the eighth-floor of a large complex overlooking the River Thames and had lived there for the past six years. It's a fifteen-minute walk from MI5 HQ. Sally doesn't own a car, preferring to hire one when the need arises. Most travel was undertaken by tube and train.

She was an intelligent and resourceful individual, who found her work both challenging and all consuming. The secrecy of her role also caused her, on occasions, to feel lonely. In recent times, she had considered resigning from the service to develop in an entirely new direction. When she returned back home to stay with her parents, in their spacious house in the country, she was back in her true identity and able to socialise with family and friends.

Much later in the evening, Julian was back at home in his cottage. He relaxed in his favoured leather chair, with a large tumbler of single malt whisky in one hand, and in the background music was quietly playing. In his mind he was replaying the events of the previous two weeks, including his American adventure and the unexpected undertaking of Operation Dragonfly on the luxurious Queen Mary 2. Plus, the added, and again unexpected, opportunity to work with Sally.

His mind wandered back to 'Mr Church' and his whispered comment: 'One of yours, I believe.' What had he meant? Was it just a throwaway, meaningless, comment of a dying man?

Julian could not let it go. He silently began to analyse the events from the beginning. The man was a professional killer. His 'sponsors' would have put much effort and expense, and good reason, to have their intended victim eliminated with the quiet disposal of the body.

Re-enacting in his mind what happened just after 'Mr Church' was shot by the two Navy SEALs. He considered:

They stood over him, satisfying themselves he was no longer a danger, then immediately left the room. They and others, who checked the room, were in full combat gear. Julian on entering the room had shouted a couple of commands. His accent would have identified him as British. He was the only one not in uniform. In that brief moment had 'Mr Church' identified him as probably with British Intelligence?

Julian poured himself another whisky and continued with his train of thought:

With their professionalism, vast intelligence apparatus and resources would 'Mr Church' have been so inept that the wrong victim was identified?

The more Julian thought about the matter the more unsettled he became. Little had officially been said about the modest man who, apparently, was not told about the events so as not to spoil his holiday!

Likewise, the identity of the 'true' intended victim was not to be pursued because Russian billionaire oligarchs, with their security and privacy, do not like to be inconvenienced by mere mortals from the Security Service. Julian would need to further consider the position. He felt unable to discuss it with any member of staff.

'Mrs Church' was now in the custody of the FBI, as was the body of 'Mr Church.' The agency would also be investigating the South African connection. Julian wondered how much feedback MI5 would eventually receive. He doubted the service would receive all the intelligence gained and, as Julian's involvement was at the end, he probably would not receive any update.

As Julian sat, in the late evening, alone in his West Sussex cottage contemplating on the previous week's events, Sally fifty miles away was in similar mode.

She was sitting on the balcony of her apartment high up on the eighth-floor overlooking the River Thames. It was a quiet still evening, with a cloudless sky. The glittering multicoloured lights from the buildings on the far side of the river, together with the lights on the passing pleasure boats, added to a feeling of calmness.

Sitting on the balcony looking out onto the river, brought back recent pleasant memories of sitting together with Julian on their stateroom balcony on Queen Mary 2. They had been employed on a serious operational matter and romance was not on the agenda, but Sally had enjoyed their time together. She thought they had much in common, and shared a similar sense of humour and values on life.

Sally recalled, with a happy smile, his comment that he thought her 'gorgeous, but a good liar.' She was hopeful their relationship would develop and, at some time in the future, be able to take Julian home to meet her parents and family. Taking a boyfriend home was not something she had done for a long time.

Julian and Sally spoke together on the telephone before retiring for the night. Earlier in the day they agreed that it would be inappropriate to telephone each other whilst in the working environment. They would keep in touch by use of their personal iPhones with calls being made during the latter part of the evening. Both had busy work schedules and anticipated being able to spend a weekend together in three weeks' time.

Monday morning arrived. Julian was back in his office at MI5 Head Quarters, London. Mark Holloway joined him, each with a mug of coffee, to discuss the events of the previous two weeks. Although Julian briefly outlined the working element of his trip to America and Operation Dragonfly, it was mainly a light-hearted comment on some of the funnier and more absurd aspects.

He also made comment on some of his faux pas and the cultural differences between the FBI and MI5. He gave an example of when he was working with the FBI in Miami: he was invited to join several agents in an early morning five-mile run along Miami Beach. Although he didn't enjoy running for the sake of it, he felt obliged to join his hosts. With MI5 secrecy and discretion of staff is paramount. So, he was a little taken by surprise when the group left the changing room to begin their run. The agents were wearing official tracksuits with FBI emblazoned in large lettering across the back of their jackets.

"From a distance of one hundred yards the public could identify it was the FBI team out for their morning exercise. Can't imagine our lot running alongside the River Thames advertising our service," he said with a deprecating laugh.

The serious debrief on his visit to America and Operation Dragonfly would take place later that morning with Director Jane Rigby. For the present, Julian would remain in his office sorting paperwork and dictating reports.

It was after lunch that Julian Lawson eventually had the meeting with Director Jane Rigby. He was now back in formal business mode. Throughout both the American visit and the operation on QM2, Jane Rigby had maintained contact with Lawson via secure email and video conferencing. So, today's meeting was to ensure all areas had been covered and that she was fully conversant with all actions and decisions that had been made. She was a stickler for detail.

Director Jane Rigby casually asked:

"How did you get on with Sally? I recall the part she played in the Land Rover exercise and your annoyance, almost to the point of anger, towards her."

"That was all forgiven a long time ago. She's a very competent, professional and caring lady. Operation Dragonfly was successful. We worked well as a team."

Lawson did not give a hint of their developing personal relationship. When they were back at his cottage, they had made a decision to withhold submitting a report to Human Resources about their budding friendship until after their planned weekend together.

Lawson had also made a decision not to confide in Jane Rigby, or any other colleague within the department, about the dying words of 'Mr Church.'

When an operational police officer, in his rank of detective chief inspector, he would deal with a major crime investigation from beginning to end: From the initial visit to the scene; to viewing the body; to liaising with the Scenes of Crime officers; to ensuring all necessary procedures and actions were correctly undertaken. Then, back at the relevant police station, he would ensure the murder incident room was correctly set up and fully functioning in accordance with national policy and his specific instructions. Throughout the investigation he would have full control, assess all incoming information and intelligence, and be the ultimate decision maker. His involvement would continue to the prosecution of the defendant before the Crown Court, and finalisation of the case after conviction.

Working with MI5 was totally different. Each department would only handle one element of a complex case. No officer would know the full story of any investigation. This was done to protect the secrecy and integrity of the matter at hand. Lawson could understand the logic. However, for a man with his police background, and experience, it was frustrating. It devalued the sense of achievement one got at the successful conclusion of a case.

His thoughts went back to some of his recent MI5 cases: Operation Backfire referred to the case of the assassin who arrived in the UK aboard a sea ferry. The subject was subsequently interviewed by Lawson with the file, then handed to the police, with other identified sensitive aspects of the case being designated to a different section of MI5.

Similarly, with the case involving the defector given the pseudonym Springwatch. Lawson would not have the opportunity to know his identity, nor be permitted to interview him. He had only been given one element of the case to investigate. Other matters would be handled by other sections.

The policy on all such cases, was that each section of the service would only be given the information necessary to undertake that element of the case. Lawson had completed his element of the case by interviewing Professor Marcus Longfellow, and one of his ex-students, Steven Archer. Other aspects were scheduled to be undertaken by other sections within the service.

With regard to Operation Dragonfly, Lawson's element of the case had resulted in a successful outcome, as far as MI5 was concerned, with him being informed his involvement in the investigation was at the end. He would move on and be assigned a new case. He would not be permitted to use the organisation's resources or facilities to conduct further investigation. Unauthorised use of telephones or record checks was not tolerated. Such use would be a major disciplinary breach with serious consequences.

Alone back in his office, Lawson continued working on his paperwork. That nagging feeling about the dead 'Mr Church' and his whispered comment 'One of yours, I believe' was back in his thoughts. He removed his reading spectacles, placed them on the desk and leaned back in his chair.

He thought of the debrief he had just had with Director Jane Rigby. She was so meticulous on detail, yet the absence of not knowing the identity of the intended victim for Operation Dragonfly did not even cause comment. Why? The senior management team had also, in his opinion, too easily dismissed the 'modest-man' as being the misidentified victim. Again, Director Jane Rigby had not felt it relevant to comment. Lawson felt compelled to look further, but he should do so with care.

That evening, back at his cottage, he sits at his desk and takes from his wallet a slip of Cunard headed note paper. It contained the details of the 'modest man' who stayed in the low-cost stateroom on QM2. The modest man, senior management decided, should not be informed about Operation Dragonfly as it might 'cause him worry and spoil his holiday.' This was the second part of the equation which, Lawson felt, did not make sense.

When the operation had been active, and they were sitting in their stateroom participating in the team video conference, he had written down the man's passport details as it was flashed on the computer screen. So, on the slip of note paper he had the man's details: Matthew William Bolton, sixty-eight years of age, with an address in Shropshire. He also has a good quality colour photograph of the man. Lawson was cautious that he should not use any of the facilities within MI5 HQ to check-out the man's details.

He was also acutely aware, that if the man had a suspicious background, any search or contact with the Passport Office or other government department might raise an 'alert' for an interested agency. That interested party, perhaps, being one of the British Intelligence agencies.

So, for the present, he would restrict himself to the normal Internet searches for Matthew William Bolton, in the age group of sixty plus, with an address in Shropshire. Lawson found the man did not appear to have a presence on Facebook, Twitter or any other social media account. Neither did the telephone details of such a person appear on the British Telecom website.

A Google Map search identified the address as being a modest terraced nineteen-sixties style house. A general Internet search inputting the man's details was negative. Often such searches identified if a person has, at any time, attracted media attention. When Lawson next had an official day off, he intended to further research the background of Matthew Bolton.

Next day, Director Jane Rigby called Lawson and Holloway to attend a meeting in the conference Silver Room. She presented them with a folder:

"Recently you both undertook an interview of Steven Archer as a consequence of intelligence being obtained from the defector with the pseudonym Springwatch. Yesterday, I received interesting intelligence concerning further espionage activities by Archer. I would appreciate you undertaking a second interrogation of this man. Senior management has asked that it be done without delay."

She placed the file, marked Secret, on the table in front of Lawson.

He turned to Holloway and suggested:

"Tomorrow morning?" Holloway nodded in agreement.

Lawson picked up the file and with Holloway walked back to his office to study and discuss the content.

As a young operational police detective constable, his old detective sergeant would often comment that the best chance of getting a 'villain' to admit a crime was to arrest him early in the morning, lock him in the cells for a couple of hours. Then the arresting officers would go for a full English breakfast. Once refreshed they would commence the interrogation. The sergeant's description was not quite that polite. Times may have changed, but the benefits of an early visit for an interrogation remained.

At 06:00 hours the following morning, Steven Archer received an unexpected knock on his door at his home in Brockenhurst, Hampshire. Opening the front door, he was greeted by Lawson and Holloway. The conversation was brief, but polite. Mr Archer was required to go with them to London for a further interview. No, he did not have a choice. The matter was urgent. They had come to collect him, which would save him the cost of the train fare and he would be given breakfast when they arrived in London.

Lawson politely said he would not discuss the matter until the interview in London. Within ten minutes, Archer was dressed, and they were in the car driving towards London. There was no conversation.

The interview was to take place in the same interrogation centre Archer had attended previously, located at the rear of Admiralty House in Horse Guards Parade. As promised, he was served a Continental breakfast and coffee. Lawson and Holloway just had coffee. As a deliberate tactic they did not converse with Archer. Lawson was of the opinion: 'Silence is often the best interrogation tool.'

Once the tray and coffee cups had been cleared away, Lawson sat behind the large solid desk and indicated for Archer to take a seat in front of him on a slightly lower chair. Holloway sat to the right side of Lawson as before.

Lawson puts on his reading spectacles and opens the folder on the desk before him. His actions were deliberately slow, calm and confident. He reiterated details of the previous interview and asked Archer to confirm its correctness. Archer nodded in agreement.

Lawson asked:

"Is that the full story or is there more you need to tell us?"

"Yes, you have the full account. I have nothing more to add."

Lawson remained looking serious:

"Yes, I know we have the full story. The question I am asking is, have you told us the full story?"

Archer looked confused:

"I've already told you everything."

Lawson responded:

"Please Mr Steven Archer. Think very carefully before you answer."

Lawson leaned forward with both elbows resting on the desk. He removed his spectacles and placed them on the desk in front of him. With his elbows still resting on the desk he clasped his hands together and gently and slowly tapped his index fingers together. He looked straight at Archer, who did not respond to the question.

Lawson remained without moving or speaking: he just looked directly at Archer. In his police role he had undertaken many long and serious interrogations, including for murder and terrorism.

Archer was beginning to look nervous. After several minutes, Lawson gave a slight smile and a nod to Archer but did not speak.

Finally, Archer asked:

"What do you expect me to say."

"The truth." Lawson retained his position and said nothing further.

Archer, hesitantly asked:

"Is it about me having a mistress?"

Lawson sat back in his chair:

"Helen? Yes, we know about her. And about the holidays you take together to your holiday home in Spain."

"Sorry, I wasn't going to mention that because I didn't think it was relevant."

"It is relevant. It takes us on the journey of how you have managed to purchase for cash a holiday villa in Spain and make frequent visits there with Helen. Our enquires show your wife, Janet, doesn't know about the villa or Helen. You simply convinced her that your job takes you abroad to work."

"Yes, I feel guilty for lying to Janet. I am incredibly careful with my money and have used my savings to buy my villa."

Lawson replied:

"One last chance. What else should you be telling us? Remember Mr Archer, what I said to you at the previous interview: we do not work on speculation or rumour, but on facts. Please think carefully."

Archer shook his head: "No, there's nothing."

Lawson remained calm and politely continued:

"Mr Archer, several facts for you to consider. You have a building society account in the false name of Brian Patrick Weller with the address being your Spanish villa. After paying cash for your villa, you still have nearly two hundred thousand Euros in the account."

Lawson placed a print-out of the account in front of Archer.

He then took from his briefcase, a clear plastic exhibit bag containing an iPhone and handed it to Archer:

"Is this your iPhone and the one we seized from you at the previous interview? Look at it carefully before answering."

Archer took hold of the exhibit bag and examined the iPhone: "Yes, it's mine."

"Who gave it to you?"

"I think I bought it from the Amazon website."

Lawson turned to Holloway and commented:

"Mr Archer still thinks we're naïve. He's heading for a big fall."

Lawson looks back to Archer, took hold of the exhibit bag and added:

"Mr Archer, this is a very elegant looking iPhone. When our analysts examined the content, there was an extra surprise. This is no ordinary iPhone. It's an extremely expensive, highly sophisticated piece of equipment. It's a one-off. A special secret camera, designed and constructed by a foreign intelligence agency. How did you acquire this piece of equipment?

Archer put his head in his hands and after composing his emotions responded:

"It was left for me at that drop-off location in the New Forest. He then gave me instructions on how to use it, during one of our telephone calls."

"How long ago was that?"

"About three years back."

"Why?"

"He suggested it might be useful."

Lawson shook his head:

"Mr Archer, you are being a very silly person. Take a deep breath and tell yourself it's in your best interest to tell the truth. We know what's been going on. We accept that initially you were blackmailed into obtaining secrets during your contract work with the Ministry of Defence. However, you saw an opportunity to make more money. You got greedy. We know you suggested to your handler that from other locations you could obtain secret documents and photographs of aircraft in development. You demanded significant cash in exchange for results. That's when you were given this sophisticated camera. Am I correct so far?"

Archer replied with a single response: "Yes."

Archer finally decided to cooperate. He was given a note pad and pen and asked to write down the various companies from which he had stolen classified documents and obtained photographs of aircraft parts under development. This continued for a further two hours.

He was eventually driven back to his home address. The following day Lawson prepared a classified report on the interview with Archer, which he handed to Director Jane Rigby.

He remained late in the office completing some necessary paperwork when he received a text message from Sally. She obviously didn't realise he was still at work, as they previously agreed not to contact each other during working hours. The message was brief. She had clearly experienced a bad day and was seeking his reassuring words of comfort. Sally's apartment was a fifteen-minute walk from MI5 HQ. He signed off duty and walked to her apartment.

Sally greeted Julian with a warm embrace. Her eyes were moist. She had been crying. He continued to hug her as they walked into the lounge and sat together on the settee. She apologised for, what she described as her 'silly girlie' behaviour, but it had been a particularly long and rotten day and she felt it would be repeated tomorrow.

She explained that several months back her surveillance team had been working long days on a terrorist related case. The conditions had been difficult, fast moving and often dangerous. The 'target' had been unpredictable and extremely surveillance aware. The work had been exhausting. The climax had come suddenly when the 'target' met up with four of his associates, produced knives and violently attacked two members of the surveillance team.

Sally became more visibly upset, as she told Julian the story. Both of her colleagues received stab wounds as a consequence of the attack. She abandoned her surveillance role and ran to their assistance. One needed urgent treatment to stem the flow of blood from a chest wound. The 'target' and his associates made good their escape but were arrested by police the following day. Her seriously injured colleague spent several weeks in hospital recovering from his injuries.

The horror of that night remained with her. When at home alone, she would often wake up in a cold sweat feeling confused and helpless. Sally gave Julian an extra hug:

"I hadn't intended to tell you about this. It is all part of the job. If I can't hack it, I shouldn't be doing it. Sorry."

"Please Sally, if our relationship is to develop, we should share our secrets and emotions. I have similar fears from my own experiences and, like you, I've never spoken about this to anyone."

She hugged his arm and reflected on their time together on the QM2. It had been their work. They had maintained a professional business relationship, but she had felt happy and secure in his presence.

Sally continued to explain that she had spent the whole day in the witness box at the Central Criminal Court in London, commonly referred to as the Old Bailey, giving evidence in the case she had just mentioned. She had felt under pressure throughout the day. When giving evidence in a court of law, the identity of an MI5 officer is protected from public view, and from the gaze of the jury.

She had been taken into the court via the rear entrance and spent the day in the witness box from behind a screen. The experience had been made worse by the unpleasant and relentless questioning by the defence barrister. He had challenged every aspect of her evidence. He had challenged her truthfulness and her integrity, and suggested some of her evidence was made up. Tomorrow, she would be back, behind the screen to continue the cross examination. She would continue to remain anonymous.

Julian tried to offer her reassurance. At times, the world can feel like a difficult and lonely place. He promised to telephone her tomorrow evening and said he was looking forward to spending their weekend together. He mentioned he had arranged with HQ to take three days annual leave, ostensibly to undertake a short hill-walking holiday.

It was just before midnight when he arrived back home at his cottage. He gave Sally a telephone call to check on her welfare. She assured him she was fine, and thanked him for his reassuring visit.

He sat down, deciding not to have a whisky, but thought about his visit to Sally. She was upset. He hadn't seen her like that before. At times it could be a stressful job and taking time out and relaxing was so important. As an operational police detective chief inspector, he would often be called on to deal with death.

On average, about once each month, he would be required to attend a post-mortem on a murder victim or a suspicious death. The unpleasant smell from the mortuary remains in the nostrils for several days after the event. Post-mortems would last between three to five hours; the work being undertaken by a skilled and knowledgeable Home Office approved pathologist.

As a Senior Investigating Officer, Lawson recalled, he would remain present throughout, answering questions from the pathologist on the circumstances of the killing. Often the pathologist would hold in his hand the heart, or some other item from the body, to explain the injury and the likely fatal blow that caused the death. Following his attendance at a post-mortem, he would inevitably feel quiet and in a reflective mood. Life is so precious.

He continued to think about Sally and the sadness she had shown this evening. Although he tried not to, his mind would not let him forget his own near-death experience in Ireland when the police car he was travelling in was ambushed:

For a moment there had been chaos and confusion. The car had come to a sudden unexpected stop. The police inspector driver lay back in his seat seriously injured from a gunshot wound. For protection, Lawson crouched low by the front side of the car. Moments earlier he had leaped from the front passenger seat of the car, with his handgun firmly clasped in both hands, and shot dead the armed attacker. The body of the young terrorist lay a matter of feet away.

Now there was just darkness and silence. A dead terrorist in front of him and a seriously wounded officer behind him. Lawson was alone. Was there another terrorist hiding in the undergrowth with a high-powered sniper's rifle, cocked and ready to kill? Crouching by the side of the police car, was this to be Lawson's last minute alive? He had shouted into his radio for assistance and remained still.

The silence was broken by the sound of rotating helicopter blades. The sound grew louder and appeared to be in stereo. He looked up at the black night sky. Racing towards his location, was a military Wildcat helicopter approaching from the right. In apparent formation, and approaching from his left, was a second military Wildcat helicopter.

The helicopter from the right, hovered high up over the stationary police car. Powerful searchlights beamed down lighting up the nearby fields and sweeping the area. A soldier, dressed in full combat gear, was kneeling by the open side door of the helicopter manning a mounted heavy machine gun.

The second helicopter quickly landed nearby. Before it had touched down, the side door was opened and several soldiers, again in full combat gear, with rifles at the ready, jumped to the ground spreading out to form a protective perimeter. Two paramedics followed to give emergency treatment to the injured police inspector. He was quickly strapped onto a stretcher and carried to one of the helicopters. Several armoured vehicles then arrived at the scene and control was restored.

Like Sally, and no doubt like many of their colleagues, Lawson experienced unpleasant flashbacks during the night when at home alone. He never mentions such things. It was in the past. He prepared for a busy day ahead.

CHAPTER TEN

An Element of Subterfuge

An extremely early start was required. By 03:00 hours Lawson was in his Land Rover Defender truck, having departed from his cottage in Petworth, and was on his way heading North-West towards his destination, Shrewsbury, in the county of Shropshire.

He had on board his camping equipment and, if necessary, has provisions for three days. The journey he was undertaking was about one hundred and eighty miles, most of which was by motorway and good class A roads. He estimated reaching his destination within four hours.

By 07:00 hours he had reached the end of his journey and parked his truck in a local council car park. The apparent home of Matthew Bolton was only a couple of hundred yards away. Lawson casually walked by the terraced house, noting the window blinds on both the ground and upper floors were drawn closed. There did not appear to be any movement in the house. The small front garden has been paved over as a hard standing. There was no vehicle on it. He walked into town and had a long leisurely breakfast and coffee at a local café.

Lawson then purchased a copy of the Telegraph newspaper and returned to his truck, where he sat reading for an hour or more. At 10:00 hours he slowly walked back past Matthew Bolton's house, noting the blinds to all the windows were still drawn closed and the parking bay remained vacant, indicating no one was currently at home.

Time to deploy an element of subterfuge. He took a piece of paper from his jacket pocket and knocks on the front door of the house, apparently, owned by Matthew Bolton. Lawson had already memorised the face of Bolton from the covert photographs taken on board QM2.

Should someone answer, Lawson would, hopefully, be able to identify if it is the man known as Matthew Bolton. Lawson's excuse for knocking on the door, would be to politely apologise for the intrusion. Refer to the piece of paper, quote a made-up name, and pretend he was looking for the person who lived in the road, but he didn't have the actual house number. As Lawson expected, from his observations of the house, there was no reply.

Lawson knocked on the door of a neighbouring house, using a slightly different tactic. When an elderly lady answered, he smiled:

"Good morning madam. I'm sorry to trouble you, but I'm trying to contact your neighbour, Mr Matthew

Bolton, but there's no reply. He's an old friend of my father and I promised to visit Matthew when I was in Shrewsbury. Do you know when he's due back?"

"No, I haven't seen him for several weeks."

"Would you happen to know where he's gone?"

"On holiday to America, to see his daughter."

"Do you know, where in America she lives?"

"I don't know."

She hesitated, then continued:

"I've just remembered. I saw David Hewitt, our local taxi driver, collect Mr Bolton from his home. That must have been when he was going on holiday. David might know when he's coming back." She gave Lawson David Hewitt's home address.

Lawson sensed the lady was willing to indulge in gossip, so continued with his questions:

"I don't personally know Matthew. How long has he lived here?"

"Must be about four years, but we rarely see him."

"Bit of a recluse, is he?"

"No, I wouldn't call him a recluse, although he lives alone and never has visitors to the house. He has an old white coloured camper van and often goes away on trips round the country."

"When at home does he park it on the hard standing?"

"Yes."

"Does he have any local friends, or go to any social clubs in the area?"

The lady nods and replies: "Not that I am aware of."

Lawson continues:

"When he's not away on his trips, and living alone, I wonder what he gets up to?"

"Once, my husband saw Mr Bolton driving his camper van out of the driveway of a big country house. I mentioned this to him, in passing, and he said he did some part-time gardening at the house."

"That is interesting. Do you know the house in question?"

"My husband said it was about twelve miles up the road. Apparently a very grand house, at the end of a long drive with tall wrought iron gates."

Lawson thanks the lady for her time and wishes her well.

He visits David Hewitt, the local taxi driver. He uses the same ploy and ascertains he took Matthew Bolton to Birmingham International Airport. He consults his records and is able to supply Lawson with the date he drove Bolton to the airport. He also recalls Bolton saying he was meeting up with his daughter for a walking holiday in America. No return date was given.

Lawson continues with his subterfuge. During his earlier internet searches, he had been unable to find any presence of Matthew Bolton on any social media platform. Perhaps, he doesn't use the Internet? With this in mind, Lawson decides to visit local travel agents.

He enters the travel agency near to Bolton's home address:

"Good morning. I'd be extremely grateful if you could help me. I've travelled up from London to visit my father's elderly relative, Matthew Bolton, to check he's ok. My father hasn't been able to contact him and is worried. I've spoken to Matthew's neighbour who said he booked a holiday to America through your office. She said he flew out on the third of last month. It's most odd that he didn't tell my father. I know it's irregular, but father is so concerned for Matthew's welfare; could you possibly check your records to see when he is due back. May I thank you in advance."

The ploy works. The representative checks her computer, but says they have no record of Mr Bolton. Lawson thanks her. He apologies and suggests 'maybe the neighbour is confused about the travel agency Matthew used.'

He uses the same ploy at two further local travel agencies, but without success.

At the fourth agency he visits, success:

"Yes, here we are. Mr Bolton flew out on the date you quote. It was an all-inclusive package to an hotel in the White Mountains National Park, New Hampshire. I actually remember Mr Bolton coming in to make the booking. He was excited about meeting up with his daughter for a walking holiday. He said she was a visiting professor at a university in Vermont, New England. She was coming to the end of her three-year secondment, and he hadn't seen her for several years."

"And the date he was booked to return?" enquires Lawson.

"He made no return booking. I recall him saying he was retired, with no rush to get back, so might stay in the US and do some touring."

Lawson thanks the helpful representative. Saying her help has eased his worry. He will now endeavour to contact Mr Bolton's daughter to confirm he is safe and well.

Lawson returns to his Land Rover. He sits for a while writing up his personal notes and thinking. It's been a fruitful morning's work. He recalls the helpful elderly neighbour describing Mr Bolton as, apparently, having a part-time gardening job at a large country house about twelve miles 'up the road.' He consults his map and identifies the road north of Shrewsbury.

He then sets off in his truck 'up the road' heading north. The elderly neighbour has given him a good description of the large country house and its grounds.

About ten miles out of town, still on the country road and heading north, he observes on his right a large country house situated at the end of a long drive. Entry is barred by tall wrought iron gates. He continues driving north for several more miles. There are no other houses that fit the description given by the elderly neighbour. He turns the car around and heads back in the direction of the large country house.

Lawson parks in a lay-by near to the house. He puts on his walking boots and his backpack. From the back of the truck, he takes out a one-gallon plastic water container, which is empty. Carrying the container, plus a walking stick, he strolls along the road and enters the drive via a small, unlocked gate just offset from the main gates.

As he nears the house he sees in the distance, parked in the rear yard, an old white coloured camper van. Could this be Mr Bolton's van? Could Mr Bolton actually be there doing some gardening?

In his mind, Lawson has a clear picture of Mr Bolton. He feels confident that, should they meet in the garden, Bolton will not recognise him as he will not have seen him on the QM2. Nevertheless, as an additional precaution, he takes a Beanie hat from his backpack and puts it on. He also notices the high-level of security cameras protecting the house and grounds.

He has a ready excuse prepared as to why he is there. He will say his Land Rover radiator has sprung a leak, which he has temporarily managed to fix, but he needs to refill it with water, before he is able to continue his journey.

Lawson knocks on the heavy oak main doors, but there is no reply. He begins to walk around the side of the house, prominently holding out in front of him the water container.

As he approaches the rear of the house two large Irish Setter dogs bound towards him. On the sun-terrace there is a man sitting in a sun-lounger holding a glass of wine. He turns and shouts at the two dogs. Lawson walks towards the man, holding out the water container and voicing his excuse for being there.

The man is not unduly perturbed by the intrusion. He walks towards Lawson, with his hand out to take the water container. There's an outside water tap nearby and he is willing to help the stranger with the leaking Land Rover. Lawson thanks him and hands over the container.

For a moment he feels lost for words. He quickly regains his composure. He has no doubts: the man filling his water container is the Mr Matthew Bolton, the 'modest-man' from QM2. He certainly does not appear to be the part-time gardener.

Lawson is handed the filled water container.

"Thank you, Sir. I do appreciate your kind help. What a lovely house. I assume you are the lucky owner?"

The man nods and with a smile responds: "Yes, I am."

"May I ask, how long have you lived here?"

"For the past five years."

"The grounds are magnificent. How many acres?"

The man is still happy and relaxed to answer the questions:

"Just over six acres of garden and a further twenty acres of woodland."

Lawson feels he can ask one further question without raising suspicion:

"Sir, do I detect a slight accent that is not from this part of the country?"

"Yes, I am originally from Poland."

More likely from Russia, Lawson is beginning to think.

Lawson, now feeling more confident, jokes that he wouldn't mind working there as a gardener. The man responds by saying he does all the gardening himself. Just final confirmation, for Lawson, that the modest 'part-time gardener' from Shrewsbury is actually the wealthy owner, standing before him, of this magnificent house.

Lawson does not intend to identify himself to the man, nor disclose he has figured out the deception. He, once again, thanks the man for his kind help and walks back down the driveway to his Land Rover truck. He decides to drive several miles away from this location.

He then parks at a motorway service station for a coffee and to think over what he has just experienced.

He logs on to the Internet and finds the website for the local estate agents. He finds details of the house he has just visited. It was sold five years ago for four and a half million pounds. Lawson decides he has achieved his mission and drives back to Petworth.

Back at his cottage, he undertakes more internet research to try to identify the man's daughter. It has been stated she is a visiting professor undertaking research at a university in Vermont, New England, coming to the end of her three-year secondment. His assumption is that she is Russian. With the information he possesses he researches faculty profiles of several universities. He believes he has identified her.

Lawson has concluded his personal research. He feels he has drawn the facts together and now has an understanding of what has occurred and possibly why:

He begins with the dying comment from the man named as Mr Church: 'One of yours, I believe' to Mr Matthew Bolton dismissed as being misidentified as the intended target. Would the assassins have made such a mistake? Lawson thinks not. Why had MI5 so easily accepted this version of events?

Lawson's research had identified that the Mr Bolton from QM2 was leading a double existence. He pretends to be of modest means when he is an extremely wealthy man living a secret life in luxury. Why?

He holds a genuine British passport, but states he is Polish, but more likely Russian. Why?

Lawson believes Senior elements within British Intelligence must have known the true facts. Why the deception?

Lawson has not used any official facilities to undertake his research. Everything has been done in his own time, at his own cost and using his own facilities to obtain data that is publicly available. Perhaps, on occasions, he has deployed a little harmless subterfuge, but no crime has been committed.

Back at MI5 HQ London, Lawson is invited to a meeting at Director Jane Rigby's office. No other persons are present. It is a large well-furnished office befitting the rank of a Director within MI5.

She invites Lawson to take a seat in the more relaxed section of her office, with its two comfy leather armchairs and low coffee table. Jane serves fresh coffee. She is keen to have a chat to check on his well-being, commenting that she is aware how busy he has been. Jane also conveys words of praise from the Director General, who is pleased with the results Julian has achieved.

Jane is aware of the three days Julian has recently taken as a walking holiday and enquires if it was relaxing and enjoyable. He thanks her for the kind, and the much appreciated, words from the Director General, and for her interest. He comments that he was enjoying sitting in the comfy soft leather chair. It reminds him of being at home in his similar leather armchair, which he refers to as his thinking chair.

He explains that his walking holiday in Shropshire gave him the opportunity to think about his life, his career and the future. He comments that life was marching on all too quickly.

When looking back, he said he remembered when and how they first met:

It was his first morning on the initial MI5 course. Jane personally welcomed him, and the other five recruits, with coffee and croissants. He had assumed she was from Human Resources and throughout the course she often joined them for morning coffee. Then several months later, when he was being assigned to his first operational role, Jane was again present serving coffee.

"And do you remember Jane, I made the crass remark about 'have they again roped you in to serve coffee.' Then, when the new team sat down and our Boss was introduced, it was you. I felt so embarrassed. Later, when I apologised, I recall your response: 'People are not always what they appear to be.'"

Jane smiles. "Yes, I do. No harm was done."

Jane asks Julian how he has found life working with MI5. She is one of the few members within the service who is aware of his police background. Julian explains that the two roles are quite different. In his police role he would deal with a case from beginning to end. In a case of murder, he would attend the scene of the crime and continue to have daily command up until, and beyond, conviction of the offender. Whereas, with MI5 he will only deal with one section of a case.

Julian also reminisces about how, as a young detective, he had worked undercover, often living on his wits, and thinking on his feet to get in and out of difficult situations and getting information by subterfuge.

He again reminds Jane of one of her quotes to him which was basically: 'you're only told what you need to know and only ask for what you need to know.' He compares this with when he would begin a murder investigation. As the Senior Investigating Officer, he would make a contract with the team. He would tell them everything and, in return, he would demand they tell him everything they had gathered during the course of their investigations. He had no time for secrets within the team: it would cause mistrust and could jeopardise the success of the investigation.

Julian is sending a delicate, but serious message to Jane.

Julian returns to his earlier comment about the comfy chair he is sitting in and compares it with his own 'thinking chair.' He mentions being at home and thinking about Operation Dragonfly and the death of 'Mr Church.'

"I've been thinking about his last dying comment, 'One of yours, I think.' What did he mean?"

Jane responds: "I don't recall that being in your report."

Julian feigning innocence, replies:

"Did I not include it? At the time I probably dismissed it. He was, no doubt, just saying that the soldier who shot him was one of ours."

Jane nods, as if agreeing.

He continues:

"I have the type of mind that doesn't like unfinished business. On occasions my imagination runs a little wild. I began thinking about the Mr Bolton, the man of modest means who was misidentified as the assassin's intended victim. Was he in fact the correct target? If so, what was the explanation? Was he a KGB defector, who had brought millions with him, and had been the subject of our Rehabilitation Programme? Then he, unwisely, arranges to meet up with his daughter in America. The regime in Russia is monitoring her and, thus, identify their 'traitor' and send out their killing team."

Julian pours himself another coffee. He gives a mischievous smile.

Jane gives a slightly quizzical smile but makes no comment.

Julian appears to change the subject. He continues talking about his holiday in Shropshire:

"I had a problem with my Land Rover breaking down."

Now back on a less controversial subject, Jane asks:

"Sorry to hear that. I hope it didn't spoil your holiday."

Julian, continuing to feign innocence adds:

"No. It was only a leaky radiator. I was able to fix it, but I needed a resupply of water. Fortunately, it happened about ten miles north of Shrewsbury near to a large country house. I walked up the long driveway and met the charming elderly owner, a Polish gentleman. We had a good chat, and he kindly filled my water container."

Jane simply replies: "That was kind of him."

Julian is not going to express himself any further. He has successfully conveyed the message and Jane understands. He is not going to ask direct questions and Jane is not about to give direct confirmation or elaborate.

Julian feels with confidence that Jane, as part of the senior management team, is fully conversant with all that has been happening. Indubitably, 'Mr Bolton' was part of the Rehabilitation Programme. When did the service know he was on board QM2 and being targeted for assassination, and why was the operation allowed to proceed? Were the Americans in the loop?

Certain questions remain unanswered, no doubt, to protect national security. That's the nature of the beast.

Director Jane Rigby remains relaxed, possibly a little impressed and also wary with Julian's ability to think 'outside the box.'

Jane makes a final comment on Operation Dragonfly and Julian's working relationship with Sally. She adds that Sally was impressed with his gentlemanly manner.

Julian laughs and comments:

"Reporting on me to my Boss, is she?"

Jane smiles:

"From our conversation you are clearly aware of some extremely sensitive secrets of this department, which I am confident you will keep. Let me give you a personal secret: I was Sally's sponsor in her recruitment to MI5. We are also related."

CHAPTER ELEVEN

Murder and Suicide?

British intelligence agencies operate under a sep-
arate legal framework from the police. MI5 is pri-
marily responsible for the protection of national
security. The protection of sensitive sources and
techniques to gather intelligence is central to the
success of any operation. It has no powers of arrest.
Law enforcement is carried out by the police. They
are the agency responsible for arrest and prosecu-
tion of anyone who has broken the criminal law.

Bill Turnbull had been a gamekeeper for over thirty
years. For most of his career he has worked on the
five-hundred-acre country estate in Southern England.
He is a robust calm, unhurried type of character who
takes everything in his stride. Beginning his working
day at the crack of dawn was normal for him. With his

faithful Labrador Retriever, Jake, he was out walking through the woodland checking the fencing and for signs of poachers, who had recently been stalking the estate's population of Roe deer.

Jake was ahead of him, lively bounding through the bracken and causing some wild pheasants to take flight. The dog suddenly stopped and began barking. As Bill walked towards the barking, he could see what appeared to be a dark object hanging above his dog. He stroked Jake on his nose to calm him down and looked up. It was the body of a man hanging by a rope from a low branch.

The man's feet were only about six to nine inches from the ground. Bill took out his sheath knife and cut the rope, with the body falling to the ground. By the condition of the body, he assessed the man had been dead for many hours.

Jake took out his iPhone and calmly dialled 999 to report a suicide. He gave the Police Control Room his details and location and agreed to wait with the body. The rural beat police constable had recently commenced his early-turn tour of duty and was directed to attend 'a suicide' at the location quoted.

Within thirty minutes he was with the gamekeeper viewing the body. Next on the scene was the local doctor, who had been called out to confirm the death. Although it was clearly evident the man was dead, a medically qualified doctor is required by law to attend the scene to certify death but, at that stage, not cause.

Hospital ambulances do not transport dead bodies, so the local undertakers were contacted to collect the body and take it to the county mortuary.

By 09:00 hours the body had been safely delivered to the mortuary, the GP was back at his surgery practice preparing for his busy morning to see his patients, and the rural PC was back at his police station cooking himself a breakfast of bacon and egg.

Following the end of his meal break, the PC would complete the necessary paperwork which, in turn, would be forwarded to the Coroner's Officer. In the jacket pocket of the dead man was a wallet containing documents, apparently, with his name and address. No keys were found in his possession.

The Police Control Room log of the death was updated to include the man's name and address. A local police officer was asked to call at the address to deliver the 'death message.' The officer would make the necessary enquiry regarding next of kin and arrange formal identification of the body.

There was no reply at the address. It was a semi-detached bungalow in a quiet rural cul-de-sac. The next-door neighbour said the bungalow was occupied by a married couple. They had lived there for several years and did not have children. She did not know the names of the couple, describing them as 'very private.' They rarely spoke to neighbours. She was aware the lady of the house left early each morning, and assumed she worked.

The enquiring PC posted a card through the letterbox, quoting the incident serial number, with a request for the householder to contact the Police Control Room.

By that evening there still had been no response to the card. An officer on the 'late-turn shift' was asked to call at the address, but again there was no response from the house. Due to a busy night, coupled with a shortage of staff, no further visit was made to the address.

An early morning visit the next day, again, failed to get a response. The Duty Inspector in the Police Control Room raised the issue with the local police station and a decision was taken to force an entry into the bungalow.

At midday, the front door was forced open. The police request card, put through the letter box the previous day, remained on the inner door mat with several unopened letters. Two police officers entered the elegantly furnished property. There was nothing amiss in the lounge and two bedrooms. The door to the kitchen was closed. An officer opened the door and stopped. There was a moment of silence and disbelief. She gestured her colleague to join her. On the kitchen floor lay a woman motionless and heavily bloodstained. They did not enter the room.

"Alpha one-six-three to Control. Reference Serial three-eight-two of yesterday. We have forced an entry. There is the body of a woman on the kitchen floor. She is dead. She has been subjected to a violent attack."

The death was recorded as a murder, with the case being investigated by the Major Crime Unit. The man found hanging in the local woodland the previous day was identified as the woman's husband. Within a matter of days, the media were informed that the two deaths were being linked as a murder and a suicide. A file was being prepared for submission to the County Coroner.

Two Coroner's Inquests into the deaths of Mary and Derek Honeywell, both aged thirty-five years, were opened and then adjourned pending completion of police enquires. This is normal procedure. Neither case raised Media interest beyond the local press. Nothing was reported in national newspapers or on television.

They were described as being a self-employed couple working together selling and renting out Spanish holiday villas. From the outset, the perceived assumption was that Mary Honeywell had been unlawfully killed, murdered, by her husband. Derek Honeywell had then taken his own life, suicide.

Sadly, most female homicide victims in the UK were killed by a partner or ex-partner.

Active police investigation in the murder case was almost at an end, with the paperwork being concluded with a file being prepared for the Coroner.

It is just before dawn, on a dark cold morning in February. There are few vehicles travelling on this quiet rural country road in Kent. The road is without lighting and has many sweeping bends. A car has crashed into a tree and is reported as on fire. It is burning out of control. No other vehicle was involved. The driver of a van, on his way to the fish market, has stopped to give assistance. He has dialled 999 for Police and Fire and Rescue Service. He did not witness the crash. The fire is out of control. He cannot see the driver or inside of the car.

The car is a classic 2008 Porsche 911convertible, but the fire has been so violent it will be difficult to identify what remains. The crash has occurred on a sharp bend. There are no visible tyre marks on the approach road to the crash. The initial suggestion is that this powerful sports car was being driven too fast, with the driver losing control as he attempted to negotiate the bend. Like the car, the driver's body is burned beyond recognition. Subsequent identification is obtained from dental records.

The driver and owner of the Porsche sports car is identified as Frazer Churchill-Brooks, thirty-eight years of age, single. He is the holder of a South African passport. He is recorded as a self-employed international trader and entrepreneur. His only British known address is a second-floor apartment in Brighton Marina, East Sussex. He also has a twenty-six-foot-long sports cruiser berthed in the marina.

Following his confirmed death, police enquiries indicate his business included dubious activities and illicit trade in small arms and ammunition. Some would call it, arms trafficking or gunrunning. He travelled the world, often visiting South Asia, including India and Pakistan.

The police undertook a thorough investigation of the crash scene and of what remained of the car. This included a forensic collision investigator trained to forensically reconstruct the collision. The vehicle's charred remains were meticulously examined, but there was insufficient left to give a definitive answer as to the car's road worthiness prior to the crash. However, the police investigation identified that the car had undergone a full Porsche maintenance service only two weeks before the crash.

The police reported to the media that the crash, and death, was not being treated as suspicious. A report was being prepared for the Coroner.

Lawson is back in his office. He opens his diary, on his desk-top computer, and sees that Director Jane Rigby has scheduled an unexpected one-to-one meeting for him with her for the whole morning. It begins in fifteen minutes. He closes the file he is working on and walks to her office.

Jane apologies for the short notice. She is seeking his advice, and police knowledge, on a delicate issue. She refers to the matter as Operation Greenfield. The sensitivity of the matter she is about to discuss is stressed. He is invited to take a seat in the comfy leather armchair, he sat in during their previous interesting chat. She makes the comment with a knowing smile.

"Julian, we are accustomed to dealing with complex and sensitive issues. This happens to be more so. At the conclusion of our discussion, I will be seeking your advice on what, if anything, British Intelligence should, or might, disclose to the police."

He responds: "Well, that has got my attention."

Jane placed two folders on the low coffee table that separated them and began to explain:

"The first deals with a case from Southern England. Derek Honeywell found hanging in a local woodland early one morning, by a local gamekeeper. He had been dead for some hours. The police visit his home and find his wife dead on the kitchen floor. She had been stabbed numerous times with a kitchen knife. A quiet respectable couple, both aged thirty-five years, and married for ten years. They were self-employed and worked together selling and renting-out holiday villas in Spain."

She pauses and touches the second file:

"This file refers to a Porsche 911 sports car crashing early one morning on a country road in Kent. No other vehicle was involved. The car crashes head-on into a tree and catches fire. Both car and driver are burned to a cinder. There are no witnesses. The Porsche had recently been fully serviced. An Inquest has been opened and adjourned pending the conclusion of the police investigation. The current assumption is that the car was being driven too fast, with the driver losing control as he steered into a sharp bend. The driver was Frazer Churchill-Brooks, age thirty-eight years, the holder of a South African passport. He was described as an international trader and had an apartment at Brighton Marina."

Jane took a further pause and poured coffee for Julian and herself.

She then continued:

"Regarding the deaths of Mr and Mrs Honeywell. The view expressed from day one has not changed. The commonly held opinion is that Mary was murdered by her husband Derek, who then committed suicide. The case has almost been finalised, with the police preparing a file for the Coroner's Inquest on a detected murder, followed by the suicide of the perpetrator."

"In the second case, the car crash and death of Frazer Churchill-Brooks, the police report being prepared for the Inquest will suggest Death by Accident, that he died as a consequence of the car crash followed by the fire."

Lawson sat back and looked to Jane. He sought the next instalment. He was not yet aware of a problem.

Jane continued:

"The car crash, and death of Mr Frazer Church-ill-Brooks, occurred two weeks after the deaths of Mr and Mrs Honeywell. Both cases received only local media attention. The Security Service was not aware of either case. Very recently we did become aware, very aware. From a sensitive intelligence source, we have been advised that the two events are linked. Julian, my initial review of the files leaves no doubt that they are linked."

She would be seeking senior-team authorisation for Lawson to lead, in the first instance, what she referred to as 'a limited enquiry.' The enquiry has been given the designation Operation Greenfield.

Jane picked up the second file:

"Mr Frazer Churchill-Brooks, international trader, was a very unpleasant and dangerous individual. His dubious activities involved arms trafficking across the world, which included supplying guns to criminal gangs in Russia. He was formerly a member of the South African Security Service but, in recent years, he had gone 'rogue' working for the highest paymaster.

Our recent Intelligence is that he carried out the murders on Mary and Derek Honeywell, on the orders of people in Russia. He first kidnapped Derek then hanged him to make it appear a suicide. He then killed Mary. She was 'sacrificed' to make it look like she had been killed by her husband and, thus, cover up his murder."

Lawson interjected:

"Now this is beginning to get complicated. Why, in the first place, did he need to kill Derek Honeywell?"

Jane picks up the Honeywell file and continues:

"To the outside world Mr and Mrs Honeywell were a respectable married couple selling and renting holiday villas in Spain. Secretly, Mr Honeywell was making extra money by allowing one of the holiday villas to be used, and equipped, by Russian intelligence. Having identified a 'target' they would lure him to the villa, and by surreptitious means involve him in sexual activity, which would be filmed covertly. He would then be blackmailed to spy for them."

Lawson asked: "So, why order the couple to be murdered?"

"That is where it becomes difficult and embarrassing. Mr Honeywell was actually on the payroll of British Intelligence. What you would call a double-agent. On our behalf, he fed false intelligence to the other-side and reported back to us on them. Somehow, Mr Honeywell's cover was blown, and the couple were assassinated."

Lawson commented:

"My immediate response is from a moral perspective. Mr and Mrs Honeywell were apparently a happy and loving married couple. Imagine what their respective families feel. Not only have they lost their loved ones, in tragic circumstances, but they wrongly believe Derek is an evil man who murdered his wife. If possible that wrong must, and should, be corrected."

He asked, "I understand both cases, i.e., the murder/suicide and the car crash, are being dealt with by the same police force. Firstly, is anyone in the police aware of MI5's interest.?"

"No. Nothing. I only became aware of this yesterday morning."

"Do you know when someone, anyone, in this organisation became aware."

"No."

"Would I be right in my assumption that I will never be told how this intelligence was disclosed."

Jane replied: "I believe it is a certainty the source will never be disclosed to you."

"I'll work on the assumption the Mr Honeywell was being handled by a unit within MI5, and that I will never be able to converse directly with them,"

Then with an uncharacteristic outburst he continued: "That is bloody marvellous. I am expected to help out, but with my hands tied behind my back."

Jane replied: "I'm sorry, but you know the rules."

Lawson suggested that there are two separate elements to consider with Operation Greenfield. In the first instance, just concentrate on reviewing and, hopefully, undertaking active enquires by having contact with the police. The role of MI5 is to gather intelligence to protect national security of the UK. The role of the police is to investigate crime, gather the evidence and then arrest and prosecution the alleged offenders.

Jane Rigby hands both files to Lawson for his personal review. She stresses, for the present, that he must not share the content with any other member of the service nor undertake any form of enquiry. She would discuss Operation Greenfield and seek authority to proceed. She further added, if permission to proceed was given, what information he would be permitted to disclose to the police would be clearly defined and limited.

Two days later the authority to make contact with the police was granted. It came with, as expected, strict limitations. The Chief Constable for the county had been informed along with his head of Special Branch. The Senior Investigating Officer for the case had been informed an MI5 officer would visit him to discuss certain aspects relevant to his investigation. Everything discussed will remain at his level and was not to be shared without permission of MI5.

Lawson was informed that the information he would be able to disclose to the SIO would be extremely limited. In essence, Lawson would be expected to obtain much information from the SIO without disclosing any sensitive or restricted intelligence held by MI5.

Once the senior-team had given Lawson the authority to proceed, he submitted an internal report politely, but forcefully, insisting that to have any chance of success he must receive a confidential briefing on how the Russian operation was undertaken.

Lawson quickly received the confidential essential briefing he had requested. He would not be given the source of the intelligence:

Mr Derek Honeywell had been slowly, and skilfully drawn into a well-constructed sting operation. Initially he had been persuaded to rent one of his villas to a group that organised sex parties. Discretion was key. For this he was paid a significant cash bonus. He was required to do no more than supply the villa. His wife was not made aware of this extra activity.

The organisers had selected the villa best suited for their requirement. They chose a luxury villa, which sleeps six, in Costa Blanca overlooking a beautiful beach. The villa was equipped with a gymnasium, large hot tub and outdoor swimming pool. It was located in its own grounds and not overlooked. The organisers would fly in the clients and supply their own staff to clean and manage the villa. Mr Honeywell was expected to stay away and just receive his usual, tax free, cash fee.

After several months Mr Honeywell was invited to sample the delights of one of the parties. The attractive young 'maids' gave him an enjoyable evening, and there was no charge. Two further free visits, as guest of the sponsors, were undertaken. Then, slowly the friendliness was replaced by mild insinuation and then threats. His sexual activities had been filmed. He was never told the full story, but he realised what he had become involved with, and there was no safe way to remove himself. However, the significant tax-free cash payments continued.

Mr Honeywell, from his own experience, was aware that sophisticated recording equipment had been covertly installed in the villa. With the system set up and running smoothly, the sponsors were now after specific 'clients' who they could trap by indulging them in sex parties.

These were people who would not knowingly attend such parties. They were men who held senior positions in various companies and institutions and who had unsupervised access to classified or secret information useful to a foreign intelligence agency.

There were various ruses deployed. First, the target would be chosen based on his position and ability to have access to the required information. Then his interests and weaknesses would be identified. Background research was thorough. In one case, the target was a keen golfer and would go away on golfing holidays with a colleague.

One day, through the Royal Mail post, he received an unsolicited advert for a golfing holiday in Spain. By simply returning the advert, with his details, he would have the chance to win a free golfing holiday. The winner could take a golfing friend. The ruse worked.

He 'won' the free holiday at this luxury villa in Spain, with free membership to a local golf club included. The individual was pleased with his prize and was enjoying the free holiday. The attractive young maid, with her seductive antics and free wine, soon ended up with them both in the hot tub.

More active nights were enjoyed, keeping the covert cameras busy. Blackmail soon followed. Rather than face possible humiliation, he began to copy and supply the required classified documents.

None of the activities that had taken place at the luxury villa on the Costa Blanca was known to the police investigating the apparent suicide and murder of Mr and Mrs. Honeywell.

Lawson visited the Major Incident Room for a meeting with the Senior Investigating Officer. He was there as a senior member of MI5. His police rank was not disclosed. He found it strange to walk into such a familiar environment wearing a visitors' badge. As soon as he walked into the Major Incident Room, he felt at home. He would have loved to have had the opportunity to log onto the HOLMES2 computer system and undertake his own research of the police murder data base. However, that was not possible.

He spent several hours in discussion with the helpful SIO. Lawson's approach was simple and straight forward. He advised the officer that some information had been received regarding sex parties taking place at one of the holiday villas hired out by Mr Honeywell. The actual villa used was not disclosed. MI5 was trying to identify if a public figure may have been involved and, thus, may have left his activities open to exposure by the Media.

The SIO was not aware of such an allegation. No mention of blackmail or involvement by a foreign intelligence agency was mentioned. Nor the suggestion that the deaths of Mr and Mrs Honeywell were both murders committed by a third person. The responses received from the SIO would prove useful for Lawson.

Lawson arranged a one-to-one meeting with Director Jane Rigby to give her his findings. Firstly, dealing with the death of Derek Honeywell. During his visit to the police HQ, he had been permitted to read the original Control Room log.

He commented:

"It was interesting, and relevant to note, from the outset the death was referred to as a suicide. The gamekeeper dialled 999 saying he had come across a 'suicide.' Throughout that was the term repeatedly recorded on the log. The police constable was directed to attend a 'suicide' as was the doctor. No police supervisor attended the scene. The doctor was keen to get back to his busy surgery, and the constable back to the station to cook his breakfast. All through the process nothing other than a 'death by suicide' was considered."

Lawson continued:

"Because it was regarded as a suicide, the post-mortem was undertaken by the local hospital pathologist. No doubt, the body would have been one in a queue of several general post-mortems he carried out that afternoon. If it had been regarded as a murder or suspicious death a Home Office approved, senior pathologist, would have undertaken the task."

He outlined his observations:

General limited toxicology tests had been undertaken and identified the presence of diazepam in his blood. The suggestion reached was he had probably taken some tablets to calm himself down. A full detailed examination may well have found the amount of the drug in his body had incapacitated him prior to death.

Most noticeably, no forensic tests had been undertaken on the soles of his shoes. The body was found hanging about a mile into the woodland. At the suggestion of Lawson, the shoes had now been examined. No trace of soil from the woodland was found. This strongly indicated that the body was carried there, thus, the involvement of another person or persons. The fingernails had not been forensically examined, because the death had been considered a suicide. His iPhone had never been found, so contacts and his diary details had not been traced.

The SIO had stressed to Lawson that his team had investigated the death of Mrs Honeywell and, by the time the death of Mr Honeywell was brought to their attention, it had been recorded and accepted as 'suicide.'

Lawson had raised his observations with the SIO, with a promise they would be the subject of further investigation.

Lawson also had observations on the murder of Mrs Honeywell. Likewise, he felt the police had from the outset considered her dead husband the only suspect in her murder. This was supported by the early comment to the Media that the two matters were being linked and they were not looking for anyone else in connection with her death.

Police faith in this assumption was further strengthened by the fact there had been no forced entry to the house, she was stabbed with a knife from the kitchen, and there had not been any search of the house, nor anything stolen.

Following Lawson's visit to the incident room, and his observations, further enquires had been undertaken with Mrs Honeywell's family and friends. A sister had a recollection that Mrs Honeywell had been upset to find one of the Spanish villas was being used for sex parties, with the knowledge of her husband. The sister had no further details. She acknowledged that she had not mentioned it before to the police, because she considered it irrelevant and did not wish to cause further embarrassment to the family.

Lawson next received a negative response to his request to make enquires regarding Frazer Churchill-Brooks. For the present, he was told he should not proceed. Director Jane Rigby suggested authority to proceed may never be forthcoming.

Perhaps time for one final subterfuge.

That evening he is home back at his cottage in Petworth. Brighton is only a sixty-minute journey away. He opens the wall safe in his study and changes over his identification documents. Ben Swan heads towards Brighton in his Land Rover truck. He arrives at Brighton Marina, parks his truck, and walks to the main office. It is closed, but the security office remains open twenty-four hours a day.

He knocks on the unlocked door and walks in. There are two security guards having their tea:

"Good evening gentlemen. I have an extremely delicate and discreet enquiry to undertake and require your help."

He flashes before them his police warrant card:

"I am detective chief inspector," he stopped then continued,

"Before I discuss this sensitive business, I should first take your names."

He looked towards the identity badges they are wearing and said:

"Thank you, gentleman."

He had successfully completed his ploy! Security guards get much pleasure in being taken into the confidence of the police. They were reassured by briefly seeing his official warrant card, with the police crest. However, it was not sufficiently close enough to read his name.

They will also be impressed that it is a detective chief inspector who is asking for their help. They have failed to realise he had deliberately not given them his name.

"Gentlemen, I am looking into the business activities of the late Mr Frazer Churchill-Brooks late of this parish. No doubt, you will have read in the local papers about his sad death in a car crash. You will also have read of his alleged dubious activities in arms dealing. That is why I am here. I understand you hold keys to all the apartments. With your permission, and in your presence, I would like a quick five minute look around his apartment."

The two security guards eagerly agree. He was taken to the apartment and let in. It had not been entered since Frazer Churchill-Brooks was last there. It is a small apartment, with little in the way of documents or paperwork. He checked the desk note pad. Several telephone numbers, plus the odd word are written on it. With his iPhone he photographed the note pad. He noted a postcode scribbled on the pad and keyed the details into his iPhone. He looked pleased but made no comment.

At his request, the two security guards took him to Mr Churchill-Brook's motor cruiser which is berthed nearby. He went aboard and walked around. He was interested in a spare coil of anchor rope on the deck, which he photographed. Then he politely called over the security guards and asked if one of them had a knife and would mind cutting a foot length of the rope for him. Again, they were more than pleased to help.

As he walked with the security guards back to the car park, he, again, thanked them for their assistance, and reminded them to be discreet.

He drove back, travelling west, along Madeira Drive passing the brightly illuminated Brighton Pier. He has fond memories of the city and had hoped to stop to walk around the famous Lanes, but it was getting late. The Pier reminds him of the successful author,

Peter James, and his crime novels with their fictional Brighton detective. He wondered if real detective life in Brighton is as portrayed in his books.

Next morning Lawson is back at MI5 HQ London. He asks for a meeting with Director Jane Rigby. He had been informed that the results were back on the toxicology tests he had recommended the Senior Investigating Officer have undertaken. The results show the amount of drugs Mr Honeywell had consumed would, more than likely, have incapacitated him before death. Thus, confirming the presence of a third person involved in his death. Rigby confirmed this was the case.

On the subject of Mr Frazer Churchill-Brooks, Director Jane Rigby said she could understand that Lawson would be annoyed that the senior-team would probably not sanction him undertaking further enquires.

Lawson assured her he was not upset. He placed on the low coffee table in front of her a clear plastic exhibit bag, which contained a single small page from a note pad. He said nothing.

Rigby, smiled and frowned:

"What is this?"

"There's an interesting postcode written on the note."

Lawson took out his iPhone and tapped in the postcode. He showed the iPhone screen to her.

The screen displayed the Hampshire home address of the late Mr and Mrs Honeywell.

Lawson did not give Director Rigby a chance to speak. He took a colour photograph from his file and placed it on the coffee table, saying:

"When I visited the Major Incident Room, the SIO kindly allowed me to examine and photograph the relevant exhibits. This is a close-up photograph of the rope used in the hanging. It is special jute anchor rope."

Lawson took from his folder another clear plastic exhibit bag containing a length of rope.

"This is a section of jute rope cut from a coil of rope currently sitting on the deck of the late Frazer Churchill-Brooks' motor cruiser, berthed at Brighton Marina. I believe it will be a forensic match with the rope used in the hanging of Mr Honeywell."

Lawson added: "Evidentially, the note and the rope will, I suggest, link Frazer Churchill-Brooks to the deaths of Mr and Mrs Honeywell. It will be for those above my pay-scale to decide what is given to the police."

Director Rigby responded:

"This is impressive. How did you come by it?"

Lawson smiled:

"I don't wish to appear flippant. I was told earlier in this case, that the intelligence was coming from an extremely sensitive source for which I am not privileged to know. I understand the need for such secrecy. May I just say, no law has been broken. My source is also sensitive."

Director Rigby gave a broad smile. Nothing further was said.

CHAPTER TWELVE

A Three-Day Weekend

It was Friday morning, the first day of his three-day weekend leave. The 'Julian Lawson' identification documents have been locked away in the study wall safe of his Petworth cottage. His city suits are also safely away in the bedroom wardrobe. This was Ben Swan beginning his day early, dressed in casual clothes and feeling relaxed. He was looking forward to Sally's visit tomorrow.

Late Spring, particularly at sunrise, is a special time of year. Ben was sitting on a bench in his back garden, with a mug of hot coffee, looking out towards his woodland of twenty-two acres. He had not felt this relaxed for some time.

His friendly robin fluttered onto the nearby wooden table and looked towards Ben. He was after his morning feed. Ben leaned down to his side; flicked open the lid of a rusty old biscuit tin and took out a handful of seed. He spread the seed out on the corner of the table. For an added treat, Ben walked over to the vegetable patch, picked up a garden fork, and dug over some soil to expose worms for his little friend.

With his coffee finished, and his friend fed, Ben picked up his walking stick to begin a leisurely stroll through his woodland. First, he walked on the uphill track to inspect the four acres of Sweet Chestnut which, during the winter months, was coppiced by outside contractors. Sweet Chestnut trees are coppiced on rotation every eight to fifteen years. It is a hardwood which is primarily used for fencing and making rustic gates. He was pleased to note that new shoots were already sprouting. Next season he will have the contractors back to coppice another section of the woodland.

Ben continued his leisurely walk through the densely wooded Sweet Chestnut section that had not been coppiced. He stopped and quietly watched, in the distance, a single grazing Roe deer. They are shy elegant animals who usually inhabit the edges of woodlands and are mainly seen at dawn or dusk. They have superb hearing and sense of smell. The deer had sensed Ben's presence and was off, bounding through the bracken on its spring-loaded legs. Wild Roe deer are frequent visitors to his woodland. He was only too aware they will enjoy eating the new sprouting Sweet Chestnut shoots. Some protection may be required.

He crossed over into the woodland area of tall mature beech trees, of which there are about ten acres. Throughout this section was spread a magnificent carpet of native bluebells. He recalls past happy times seeing his young nephew running through the bluebells chasing butterflies.

Ben looks up into the tall overhanging beech trees. The rooks are nesting.; large, black-feathered birds that collectively nest in the tops of trees. They are intelligent creatures. When he is working in the woods, and leaves food nearby, the birds will often invite themselves to a snack. He recalled, with a smile, the occasion a rook tried to fly off with a stolen banana from his open lunchbox.

By now, he had reached his log cabin. He unlocked the double doors and entered. The interior contained a small table and two chairs, plus a single pull-down bed. On the table sat a brass oil lamp which, when lit, of an evening gives out a pleasing warm glow.

On one wall was a large white notice board covered with coloured photographs he has taken. Photographs of his family and friends enjoying themselves in his woodland. Photographs of campfires and overnight stays. Photographs of simple happiness. Most importantly, photographs of Lucy smiling and happy: Lucy, his late wife.

For the first time since Lucy died, he looked at the wall of photographs and didn't feel sad. They made him remember happy days, happy fun days together with Lucy. Just before her passing she made Ben promise he would again find happiness. He quietly looked at her photograph and said, 'thank you.' He locked the cabin doors and walked back to his cottage. He took the opportunity to think more about his life and future.

Back in his cottage, he decided it was time for another fresh coffee. With coffee mug in hand, he walked around his study and living room. The house was well furnished and neat, just as Mrs Graysmark his housekeeper had earlier commented. It was also devoid of any photographs or personal memorabilia, again, as she had also observed. Yes, Mrs Graysmark, you're right. My house is 'sterile' of personality. Time for change, thought Ben.

Since joining MI5, Ben's contact with his previous circle of friends had virtually ceased. As had meeting up with his police colleagues. His reasoning, or initial excuse, had been his work in counter-terrorism and MI5 made that difficult. Perhaps, there was also a deeper reason. The loss of Lucy had made it difficult for him to mix with friends they had shared together.

Life was too short and precious to hide away. He recalled an MI5 colleague commenting about his own secretive role in the service: 'I'm always present, but never there.' Perhaps, that is also an echo of Ben's life.

He thought more about his current strange existence. He spends the majority of his life being Julian Lawson. Living a lie, allegedly, for the good of national security. He worked long hours, with a great bunch of colleagues, relying on their professionalism often in difficult and dangerous situations. Together they share major secret intelligence. Yet, in that whole large building, called MI5 HQ, he doesn't know the true identity of one single person.

He doesn't know the true identity of the 'good guys.' Likewise, he doesn't know the true identity of the 'bad guys.' He reflected back on recent cases: The dying 'Mr Church' he knelt down beside on Queen Mary2, who was he? Was he prepared to kill another human being for his ideology or for money? Then, there was the

'Mr Bolton.' Ex-KGB, but who is he? And, Aleksander Kozlowski, the assassin he first met on the Saint Malo to Portsmouth ferry? The same question can be asked in respect of the majority of people Ben has come into contact with since joining MI5.

On Operation Dragonfly, and working in the luxurious environment of Queen Mary 2, he had maintained a professional business-like relationship with Sally but, throughout 'deception' was present, which he disliked.

They had spent a pleasant evening dining in the Britannia Restaurant, sharing a table with two other couples, who were telling genuine stories of their families. Everything he and Sally had said in return were untruths. He had found that distasteful. The woman he shared that pleasant evening with, Sally, he did not even know her true identity.

As a detective chief inspector, whether he was dealing with the 'good or bad guys' he invariably knew their true identities. He led many murder investigations and, at the outset, would know the true identity of each victim. In each case he would meet the family of the respective victim and offer condolences, but then move on to the next case.

It was only after the death of his wife, Lucy, that he understood the long-term sadness relatives experience with the loss of a loved one. He was recently reminded of this, when he was with Director Jane Rigby discussing the deaths of Mr and Mrs Honeywell, who had been brutally murdered by Frazer Churchill-Brooks.

Ben took out his iPhone and made a call to his old and close police colleague Ray Roberts. They had joined the service about the same time and worked together as young, uniformed officers on the beat. They had been each other's best man at their respective weddings but, embarrassingly, Ben had not been in contact with Ray since Lucy's funeral.

Having successfully made contact with Ray, Ben got into his Land Rover truck and drove over to Chichester to visit Ray and his family. He had a relaxing happy afternoon catching up on the missing years. Ben, naturally, didn't refer to his existence with MI5. He briefly said that he has an office-bound role on secondment with the Home Office.

It was now late afternoon with Ben back at his cottage. He felt exhilarated at having visited his old friend and family in Chichester. He took a package from his desk drawer and set out on another walk.

He strolled through the Petworth Estate deer park towards the home of Mr and Mrs Graysmark. The couple were sitting in their back garden, enjoying the sunshine. Christopher had a glass of brandy in his hand. They welcomed Ben on his unexpected visit. He took a seat opposite them. He declined a glass of Christopher's usual brandy but accepted Helen's offer of a glass of elder flower wine.

"I've been away on a business trip to America. It was most successful. The main client was pleased to see me and was extremely helpful. I just happened to have some business to sort out at the British Embassy in Washington and I thought you might like a little present."

Ben handed the package he had been carrying to Christopher. Christopher unwrapped it, and gave a broad pleasing smile, before passing it to his wife Helen.

Helen held the present and smiled approvingly.

"Thank you, Ben. This is lovely"

It is a framed photograph of Ben, standing in the grounds of the British Embassy in Washington with the Ambassador. The photograph has been endorsed to 'Christopher and Helen' with the signature of the British Ambassador.

Christopher smiled and commented:

"I remember my time there with great affection. I'll be discreet and won't ask you what you were doing there."

Ben made a light-hearted comment to Helen:

"I have been thinking about your observation, that there are no photographs or personal ornaments in my house. It's about time I change that. So, in the future, there will be some photographs on display for you to dust."

It is a brief visit. He gave both a friendly hug and commenced the pleasant walk back through the deer park. The park is a lovely quiet place to be. Normally, he would walk straight back to his cottage.

Today he felt different. He stopped for a drink at the Badgers, a small eighteenth century, privately owned free house. It was originally called the Railway Inn. Petworth town no longer has a railway link. Ben ordered a pint of best bitter and sat down at the bar. There were several regular customers at the bar, and he entered into conversation with them. He acknowledged that he lives nearby, but has never before visited the pub. He assured them it will not be his last visit. The pub has a pleasant friendly atmosphere. He returned home to prepare for Sally's visit.

Ben was pleased that it was a warm, sunny, Saturday morning. He was up early, making sure everything in his cottage was in order and tidy. He had even purchased flowers from the local florist and had them displayed in a vase on the sitting room table.

Sally arrived, as arranged, just before midday. She was driving a hired metallic navy-blue Mini Cooper car. He welcomed her with a gentle affectionate hug. Over the past few weeks, they have been keeping in regular contact via late evening telephone calls. After a short chat, and coffee, he drove her in his Land Rover truck to, what he said is, a friendly pub nearby.

As they approached the small town of Pulborough, he turned right and down a track to a picturesque old coach house, now called the White Hart inn. It has an outdoor garden area set out with wooden tables and chairs, and fronts onto the river Arun. Several canoes were tied up against the garden's small wooden jetty, and bobbed gently in the tidal river. There were several customers already having lunch.

Sally playfully remarked:

"I remember this place. Sometime back, I came here with a group of friends."

Ben smiled but, for the present, keeps his powder dry. He didn't reply.

They entered the inn, ordered drinks and selected a ploughman's lunch from the menu. They took their drinks into the rear garden and sat at a table, to await lunch being served. It was the perfect weather for enjoying a quiet outdoor lunch in the countryside.

Sally hugged his arm and said:

"Julian, this is lovely. I'm so happy we've come back to the place we first met."

He moved his head closer to her and, continuing in a playful mood, responded:

"I first came here with a young lady I was trying to help. Her car had broken down. I invited her here for lunch, while she waited for her uncle to rescue her. She said her name was Lucy. I thought she was charming. Then I find everything, yes everything, she told me was a lie. She even had her friends watching my every move and, using a drone, took photographs of us."

Sally attempted to interrupt.

He gently tapped her nose and continued:

"No. I haven't finished. I'll give her credit for later apologising. Then, recently I was on Queen Mary 2 dining in luxury with a young lady. She called herself Sally. I looked across the table at her in evening dress and thought. she scrubs up well."

Sally gently punched him and tried to speak.

He, again, playfully, grabbed her wrist and continued:

"Actually, I thought she was gorgeous. But, and there is a big but, she was such a liar. Everything she said was fiction. What's a man to think?"

Sally, with a smile, replied:

"Not everything I say is a lie."

"OK. Is your real name Sally?"

"No. You know it isn't, but…"

He put his hand up to stop her continuing:

"I'm aware of at least two secrets you've kept from me. Firstly, your name. Secondly, you never told me my Boss, Jane Rigby, was your granny."

"She is not my granny. Jane is my aunt."

Ben smiled: "Thank you for telling me. I was wondering about her relationship to you."

Sally shook her head and laughed. "You're incorrigible."

Ben looked at Sally:

"Recently, I've been thinking a lot about my life. From now forward, when not in the employment of MI5, I am Ben Swan. I very much want you to be an important part of my life."

Ben looked directly into her blue eyes and held his right hand out towards her hand:

"Good afternoon gorgeous lady. My name is Ben Swan. What's your name?"

"This should be easy, but it isn't." She hesitated and gave a nervous smile. The decision was made. With humour, and a more confident grin, she shook Ben's hand:

"I'm pleased to meet you, Ben. My name is Emily Braithwaite."

Ben gave Emily a close, tight cuddle. Then holding her gently by her shoulders pulled back, looked into her eyes, smiled and asked:

"Is that really your name? The true name on your birth certificate? One hundred percent Emily Braithwaite?"

"Yes. Yes, to all three questions."

Ben joked: "That presents me with a big problem." With his index finger he appeared to be writing something out in his mind.

"What's the problem. Don't you like my name?"

"No, it is a lovely name but," he feigned looking serious and continued:

"The large tattoo across my back, multicoloured and in gothic script, says 'I love Sally Chambers, true.' Now I'm trying to work out how I can have it altered to read 'I love Emily Braithwaite, true.' It could be tricky."

The hugging and light-hearted banter continued over their ploughman's lunch. They spent the afternoon with Ben showing Emily around the small historic town of Petworth. In the evening he walked with her to the nearby Badgers Inn for a quiet drink which they took sitting in the rear garden with its small coloured sparkling lights strung out in the trees.

Sunday morning arrived. It was another sunny, warm and pleasant day. Ben prepared an early breakfast with Emily helping in the kitchen. He was enjoying having her company. It had been a long time since he shared his home with another. Emily was keen for Ben to meet her parents. She hadn't visited them for many months.

They set off after breakfast, in her Mini Cooper, to drive to her parent's home in the Cotswolds. It was just over a one-hundred-mile journey which Emily estimated would take about two hours. They took the pleasant country route up the A272 to Winchester and on to the A34.

Her parent's house is located a few miles beyond Cirencester. It's a substantial, six-bedroom detached property, built in local yellow/cream coloured Cotswold stone, with significant woodland and farmland. They parked in front of the triple oak built, detached garage in the rear yard. As they walked across the yard towards the main front door, an elderly man could be seen gardening. He turned and gave a friendly wave to the couple. Emily smiled and waved in return.

Ben asked, "It that your father."

Emily replied, "No, that's Giles, the gardener."

They walked towards him for Emily to stop and say hello.

Giles smiled and commented:

"It's such a pleasure to see you, my Lady. We don't see you much now. My wife often asks after you. You must have a busy life working in London."

They exchanged more pleasantries with Giles and then continued their walk to the main entrance.

Ben stopped their walking and turned to Emily:

"What did he call you?"

"I've known Giles and his wife since I was a little girl. They have various pet names for me. What did he call me? I didn't pick up on the name he used."

"Giles called you 'my Lady' is that a pet name or a title?"

Emily responded:

"It's a title. Something I rarely have cause to use. Giles is from the older generation and tends to use our titles when addressing the family. My father is an Earl. My parents are a lovely informal couple and will expect you to call them David and Diana."

Ben held Emily's hand a little tighter but didn't make any comment.

She, mischievously pulled him closer:

"I suppose that will cause you a further problem. Now you'll have to add 'Lady' to the altered tattoo on your back."

Holding his hand, Emily took Ben into the house to meet her parents. As Emily had described them, David and Diana were a friendly and relaxed couple. They had lunch together, with Emily keen to catch up on family gossip. It had been almost a year since she had visited home, although mother and daughter endeavour to keep in touch via a weekly telephone call.

Following lunch, Emily took Ben for a stroll around the extensive grounds of the house and beyond to the family dairy farm. In response to his questions, she explained that her father refers to himself as semi-retired but keeps a firm grip on the management of the farm. He is also entitled to take his seat in the House of Lords but doesn't now enjoy the pomp and ceremony involved so rarely attends.

Ben asked: "Do your parents know you work for the Security Service?"

Emily gave a long reply:

"It's known as discretion. The family roots are in public life. A long history of senior military and government service. When I was growing up, I had relatives in senior positions but, as a child never really understood their roles and I cannot recall it being discussed. We would get together for family parties, which I remember as happy times, but work was not discussed.

My family know I have a busy life in London. I'm sure they have an inkling. However, questions are never asked. I sometimes wonder about the background of my father. Beyond knowing he was in the military, he's never told me, and I've never asked."

On the return journey both agreed they've enjoyed an incredibly happy weekend and were looking forward to a future together.

Ben explained that for the past three years, since being a member of MI5, he had deliberately cut himself off from his police colleagues. Operating under a new identity presented difficulties, which Emily would understand, and this was the reason he often gave himself for not contacting police friends.

In recent weeks, perhaps even months, he'd been thinking about his current life and his future. He smiled at Emily and acknowledged her influence on his thoughts and of their growing relationship. He understood the need to protect the individual and national security, but now felt he'd had enough of the secret existence. Ben said he wished to be Ben Swan full time, not just on his days off. He'd not attended any police related function since joining MI5. In the future he intended that to change.

Ben said he'd recently heard that his first detective sergeant, when he joined the CID, had died. The DS had subsequently reached the rank of inspector. It was now Ben's desire to attend the funeral:

"I will attend as myself, detective chief inspector Ben Swan. I'd like you to attend with me, and to introduce you to my friends as my lovely girlfriend, Emily Braithwaite."

Emily replied: "I'll enjoy meeting your friends."

"It will be a traditional police funeral befitting a retired thirty-year-service officer. Many dear friends and former colleagues will join the officer's family at their local Norman church in West Sussex."

Ben explained the coffin would be adorned with a police drape with the force's crest. The officer's cap, with his folded brown gloves, would be displayed on top of the coffin. Based on previous funerals of retired police officers, during the service several colleagues of the deceased would speak with eloquence, and humour, about his dedication and pride for the force and public he served. Ben hoped that Emily will witness, at first-hand, the Police Family at work and play. He was happy that Emily was going to be part of his future.

It was late evening, with a dark, almost black, overcast sky by the time they arrived back at Petworth. Emily drove her Mini Cooper down the short track and stopped at the closed five-bar wooden gate to Ben's cottage. He got out of the passenger seat of the car and walked to unlatch the gate. It was his intention to invite Emily in for a coffee before she began her return journey.

As he leaned forward to unlatch the gate, the automatic motion sensor of the flood-light, fitted on the front of his cottage, was activated by his arrival. The bright penetrating light cast a broad beam across the gravel driveway and over his parked Land Rover Defender truck. Ben slowly pushed the heavy wooden gate open, calmly looking towards the cottage and the immediate surrounding area. He sensed that all was not well.

His profession and experience sensed danger. The gravel on the ground, at the rear of his parked truck, had recently been disturbed as though someone had been on their back inspecting the underside of the vehicle. The side gate to the rear garden was slightly ajar. Ben knows he'd left it closed. Some garden furniture had been moved, only slightly, but it had definitely been moved since he left the cottage earlier in the day. The plants growing under the front sitting room window had recently been trodden on. Without doubt, in the last few hours he had had unwelcome visitors.

In the few seconds it took him to push open the gate, a rush of possibilities flowed through his mind.

Why had someone been looking under his truck? Had an explosive device been placed under the vehicle? He was aware that he remained a target following the shooting in Ireland.

During his time with MI5, he had dealt with killers, assassins and spies, all with associates capable of seeking revenge. Perhaps, it was just potential burglars or poachers taking an interest in the cottage?

His professional instinct identified the most likely option. He senses real danger.

Emily's safety was paramount in his thoughts. He must quickly, and quietly, remove her from the likely danger. His legally held handgun was locked away in the study wall safe. Taking possession of it would be the second action he proposed to undertake.

His first action was to walk back to Emily, who was still sitting in her Mini, and speak to her:

"Emily darling, would you mind if I don't invite you into my cottage. I'm not feeling too well. Please remember, I love you very much."

Emily smiled and, through the open car window; gave him a goodnight kiss. He remained standing at the gate, ensuring that she safely drove back onto the country road and began her journey back to London.

Ben, with keys in his hand, cautiously walked towards the front door of his cottage. Once in his home, he would unlock the wall safe and take out and load his handgun. It's a German manufactured Glock 19; the type favoured for undercover operations. The gun is small and light with excellent stopping power, and with a magazine containing 15 rounds. He's aware the night could prove difficult and dangerous.

The End

Printed in Great Britain
by Amazon